I Hear the

REAPER'S
SONG

I Hear the
REAPER'S
SONG

Sara Stambaugh

Good Books
Intercourse, Pennsylvania 17534

Published by Good Books, Intercourse, PA 17534

Design and cover illustration by Craig Heisey.

"Siloam" and " 'Tis the Harvest Time" are reprinted by kind permission of Herald Press from *Church and Sunday School Hymnal,* musical editor J. D. Brunk (Scottdale, Pa.: Mennonite Publishing House, 1902).

I HEAR THE REAPER'S SONG
Copyright © 1984 by Sara E. Stambaugh
International Standard Book Number: 0-934672-24-5
Library of Congress Catalog Card Number: 84-81141

To

Silas N. Hershey
b. Mar. 22, 1881
d. Nov. 20, 1970
Aged 89 years, 7 months, and 29 days

I.

Except for that wild old doctor in the other bed who raves some and wanders up and down the hall looking for his family, it's peaceful here at Landis Homes. It's a Christian home run by the Mennonite church. Most of the nurses dress plain in the Mennonite way, and Biney's just down the hall. She's almost the only cousin I have left, but she's still a high stepper, if she is going on ninety-three. Biney brought her own furniture with her, and she rocks in her painted chair when I look in. If I miss, she's here in a wink to check things out and ask why I haven't been to visit.

Biney and I don't talk about the accident. Nobody does, but it's still with me, even if I was only fifteen back in 1896 when it happened and Biney was seventeen, just eight months older than Barbie. They were good friends—same age and first cousins—and the farms neighbored. Neither one of us ever forgot, even if we don't talk about it. It's been with me all my life, but here in the Home looking out the window across the fields, I seem to remember it better than all the rest of my life that happened in between.

Now that it's April and the fields are green again, I keep thinking I smell trailing arbutus and going through that year over again in my mind, I can't believe it all happened almost seventy-five years ago, even if everything has changed since then.

The next April everything was different, but that year we were happy the way we used to be in the spring when the wheat was up and the last of the tobacco had been stripped and sold and was ready to be hauled off to the warehouse. Pap had a buyer for his money crop (though prices were still so low that he said he'd get more from it if he smoked it himself), and the new bed was sprouting in the flats under the muslin behind the barn. The orchard behind the house made the ground white with apple blossoms, and there was hazy green all over the fields when you looked down towards the road and across to where the valley ended in a black line of trees on the south ridge. It was mostly too soon to do much to the fields except spread manure, but even that smell was sharp and good because it meant we'd soon have corn and tobacco and hay and wheat again all over our ninety-four acres. When Pap asked did anyone want to go along to Levison Hollow to fetch wood from the woodlot, even Martha scrambled to get ready, because it was good to feel the spring, and Pap said the arbutus should be out.

There were only four of us home that spring. Of the thirteen, the two babies born silent didn't count (except with Mammy) or my two little sisters Mary and Ellen who died in the scarlet fever epidemic when Martha almost died too but got off with being frail and having a deaf ear. Mammy always fussed over Martha after that, I guess because she was afraid she'd lose another and couldn't bear it, though Hen said much as Martha pampered herself she'd outlive us all. Barbie was born a couple months after my little sisters died, so dimpled and happy that Pap said God must have sent her to put some sun back in Mam's life, and he gave her Mam's name. Mam lost the second of the babies the next year, and I was born in 1881, the last of the brood. Only Hen, Martha, Barbie, and I were home that spring because the oldest four were all married and raising families of their own, and my brother Mart had gone out west to work wheat fields in the Dakotas.

That April day I went out with Pap to hitch up the wagon while Mam and the girls finished the dinner dishes and put on their wraps. Hen came out to the barn with us, but he shuffled his feet and said he guessed he wouldn't come along if Pap could manage without him. "I got to run down to the Gap," he said. Hen was twenty-four and the oldest still at home and single, old enough that Pap let him have a pretty loose rein. Pap didn't even look around from where he was settling the collar on Ben Gray, the big lead mule, to say he guessed we'd manage. He paused, though, to ask if by any chance Henry was planning on taking the courting buggy. Hen grunted, and Pap went back to fitting on the harness. "In that case, Silas," he said to me, "you'd better hitch up the spring wagon so your mother and sisters have something to ride in."

Till we came clattering down the barn hill and around beside the house, me in the spring wagon and Pap balanced on the axle of the big farm wagon we'd hoisted the box from the day before, Hen and the buggy were already halfway out the lane. "Where's he off to?" Mammy asked while Pap helped her to climb up to the wagon seat. "Off to the Gap," Pap said, and Martha gave a look to Barbie. "He's going to see that girl," she said and puckered her mouth like she was sucking a lemon before she climbed up beside Mam on the spring wagon. "No need for anyone to fuss except Silas," Pap said in his calm way. "It means he'll have to put in some work this time," and Mammy and Barb both laughed.

Pap had planned on driving the mules and sending the women ahead in the spring wagon, but Barb asked could she ride on the farm wagon and I asked could I drive it. Pap nodded and told me to mind the downhill parts before he climbed up beside Mam and Martha. Barbie and I made a run and jumped up on the big empty frame behind the mules, her balancing on the beam down the middle and me standing astraddle on the axle, fifteen years old and proud to be standing up there and driving Pap's gray mules. In the spring wagon Pap clicked to the horse, and we were off, jolting out the lane and then east down the valley towards the woodlot.

It was a rough ride because work wagons didn't have springs, and roads weren't macadamed in those days. Every time we hit a bad bump Barbie bounced and giggled, enjoying the hanging on as much as I enjoyed keeping my footing and standing tall behind the mules. Up front on the wooden seat of the spring wagon Mammy and Pap bounced too, Pap tall and straight and jolting up and down like a pump ram, and Mammy fat beside him and heaving over the bumps like the waves we saw off the boardwalk when we visited my sister Lizzie at the seashore. Martha was tiny beside them, straight as Pap and short as Mam but holding herself so stiff she hardly even moved, as if she'd glued herself onto the wagon seat.

Mammy was fat, I guess, but we liked her that way, with her round face and long Buckwalter nose and wide mouth always ready to smile unless she was worried over us kids or pretending to be mad. I still hugged her sometimes. Pap would, too, and say, "Silas, when you pick a woman, you have to look for one like this with some speck on her, not some bag of bones too skinny to heft a hayfork." Mammy would laugh and tell him to get on, or else she'd say she'd known a thing too and how to pick a handsome man. She hoped she'd taught her daughters to do as well, she'd say. Mam was a smart manager and ran the house and garden and dairy so Pap never had anything to complain about, and she knew how to help in the fields at haying and harvest, too, strong and steady as she was. If she was soft on anything, it was us kids, after losing the two babies but especially my two little sisters to the scarlet fever.

Pap didn't fuss over us like Mammy, but in some ways he was as soft as she was and liked to see us kids having a good time, maybe because his pap had been a minister, though he died before I remember. I never could imagine what it would be like having a Mennonite minister for a pap, though if old Grandmother Hershey was any indication, I don't think I'd have liked it and always figured my grandfather must have been as scary as she was, lying big and white at Uncle Elias's in the front room. They used to say Pap took after her, but I could never see it except in his being such a big man, though even at fifteen I was almost as tall as he was. They said I took after the Neffs and my mammy's mam, but I've always liked to think I took after Pap, because he was the kind of man a kid wanted to be like when he grew up.

Whoever Pap took after, I wouldn't have complained about following him down the Strasburg Road towards the woodlot or anywhere else, even if I knew he only let me drive the mules because he was ahead in the spring wagon so I couldn't run them. Down the road we went, past the Blackhorse Hotel and the voting booth and on down beyond Uncle Menno's farm and further on past my brother Enos's, to where the south ridge started easing closer to the road and the railroad came close on the other side. We turned off then, and the mules started to strain some uphill into the woods that always seemed like a green fence stretched across the world and shutting off the south, though the funny thing was, just about any direction you looked, you could see a ridge off in the distance somewhere or other, shutting you in. Some people lived on the ridges, especially to the south near the Nickel Mines, but they weren't our people, and when we got into the trees I could see Pap looking around sharp, his short winter beard outlined against the woods. The road dipped down through a hollow filled with skunk cabbage before we started to climb again. We passed a couple tracks into the woods where shacks showed through the spring growth, and Pap called back, "I hope those hillians haven't put any shanties up on my land!" Finally he pulled up beside our section of woods, and we all climbed down, Mammy and the girls to rummage through the woods for poke and arbutus and anything else they could find, and Pap and me to work.

Pap and Hen had been out in the fall and cut down some trees to season over the winter, and our job now was to haul them home. It was hard work to heat a house on wood. I don't know why nobody used coal, except because we'd have to buy it, but wood it was, for the cookstove in the kitchen, and the Franklin stoves in the front rooms, and the fires in the washhouse so Mam could do her baking. Seemed as if as far back as I could remember I'd been splitting wood and hauling it inside to the woodbox, every day, from the time I wasn't any higher than the axe handle. That was kids' work, but hauling logs was men's, and I didn't complain, pleased as I was to be taking Hen's place.

When I got back to the women they were sitting on a log, Mammy heavy and squat, and the two girls on either side of her, all of a size with their heads level, but Martha sitting straight and prim as if she was in church and Barbie restless even when she was sitting still, jiggling her toe against the grass. Her calico apron showed under her short coat, and she had a lapful of arbutus. She was fiddling with a piece, studying the waxy flowers half pink against the dark green of the leaves and lifting it now and then to smell it. Mammy was holding a piece, too, and had a basket at her feet partly full of sassafras bark and other things she liked to give us for spring tonic.

Martha was just sitting with her hands folded and looking cold. Arbutus is about the sweetest thing I know, and I could smell it when I got close, but Martha didn't have any smell after that epidemic when she was a baby. Pap used to say she was missing some of the best things in God's world, but she never acted like she cared much. She was thin like me, and Mam was always trying to fatten her up so she'd be healthy and strong like Barbie. Pap said she'd get some appetite if she went out and worked in the fields like the rest of us, but he never said it very loud, because Martha was bossy even then, and Barbie was sure to speak up too, not talking sharp but pained and hurt. None of us wanted to hurt Barbie. We all knew that different as they were, they stuck up for each other.

The three of them were talking about Barbie's young man and didn't pay much mind to me when I plunked down beside Barb on the log. "I don't know what you have against him," Mammy was saying while Barbie pulled off a flower and rolled it in her hands to make the smell stronger. "He's steady and comes from a good enough family. You'll look a bit before you'll find another one with a pap ready to buy him a farm of his own as soon as he finds the wife he wants. And he's good-looking, too. Barbara, don't you think he's good-looking?"

"Yes," Barbie said, as if she wasn't convinced, and then "No" when Mam asked if she knew any other young men around better than Enos. "I know all that, Mam," Barbie finally said with the voice she used when Mam told her some medicine would be good for her but wasn't convinced the cure was worth the dose. "I know Enos would make a good husband."

"Then what do you have against him?" Mam asked her. Martha spoke up then. "She just doesn't like him, Mammy," Martha said, "and I don't think he's good enough for her anyway." Barbie looked up from the arbutus in her lap as if what Martha said might not be quite accurate and she wanted to set the record straight. "Well, I like him all right, I guess," she said, sticking a foot out to touch a laurel bush near the log. "It's just that he's not much fun. When I'm with him all he does is pester me and talk about getting married."

Mammy seemed not to notice the pestering part and only hear the part about getting married. "I can't see what's wrong with that," she said. "Now if it was Silas here busy courting, it would be different," and we all laughed. But Barbie still looked serious. She lifted her hand and smelled where she'd rolled the arbutus. "I guess I want to do more before I settle and join church and raise a family," she said. "I don't know what, but I'm not ready for Enos, Mammy, and that's all there is to it."

Mam sighed as much as to say she'd never understand young people, but before she could say more, Pap came out of the woods, and Barb gathered her apron and jumped up to meet him. "Pap, Mammy's trying to marry me off again," she called. Pap smiled. "Well, Mother, I guess she's not an old maid yet, when she hasn't turned eighteen," he said, and we all laughed again.

It seems as though I remember us all laughing a lot in those days, especially Barbie. If I was the baby of the family, Barbie was the pet, the one all the laughing came from that I think about in the spring when I know the arbutus must be out and remember how it smelled. But it seems like we were all happy then, before all the changes.

◇ *8*

II.

Sitting here in the Home, it could be I remember things better than they were. I remember how tired I got helping Pap and Hen saw up those logs and how much splitting I had to do to get them down to stove size. But I think more about how much fun we had, and especially all the visiting and running around we got done. Sundays we always had company for dinner (unless we were invited to someone else's place), but people got around evenings, too, and even some afternoons.

Pap's next older brother, Uncle Elias, farmed the home place where my Granddaddy Hershey lived before he died, just down the path through the back meadow and across the Blackhorse Road. It seemed as though my cousin Biney was always over at our place, maybe because out of that batch she was the only one still at home except her brother Dave, who spent all his time with Ella Wilson, the girl he married the next winter. Her full name was Sabina, of course, but I don't remember anyone ever calling her that. Sabina was too fancy a name for such a catbird, Pap said. He always pretended to groan when he saw her scurrying down the barn hill or flying through the yard gate, and Mammy would say, "There goes the rest of the day's work."

Biney would bang the kitchen door shut—if she remembered to close it at all—, drop her coat on a chair, and shout, "Aunt Barbara, I have something I just got to tell Barbie!" Then the two of them, Barbie and Biney, would put their heads together and whisper and giggle till Mammy said it sounded like a squabble in the chicken coop, and Pap would ask Biney which young man she'd set her cap on this week.

"Uncle Peter," Biney would say, "you know it's leap year, and I got to do what I can while I got time." Biney wasn't much over five feet, same size as most of the women, but she was thin like the Hersheys and carried herself straight like Martha so she seemed taller. I wasn't of an age to notice looks much, at least in a first cousin, but Biney wasn't bad looking, as I remember, with the little hook most of us Hersheys have in our nose, so she looked half dignified till that mouth got going. Biney had a mouth on her, and as sure as she opened it, it was going a mile a minute with never a thought over what anybody would think. Every time she came over she was full of some party or meeting or other and bent on working out some scheme for getting there. She always asked Martha to come along, I suspect because Aunt Annie told her to, but Martha generally turned up her nose, saying the night air didn't agree with her and she had to watch her health.

Lots of weekends there were parties—crushes, they called them then, with whoever was having them pairing young people off with each other—and there were other things to do week nights, like the singing school over at

Gordonville or the sewing circle Mary Mellinger started up at Paradise. Biney managed to sample just about everything, though she didn't stick to the sewing circle very long. Her mam gave her enough sewing at home, she said, but Pap asked her how many young men were sewing in the Paradise circle and teased her about devotion to charity till Mammy shushed him and said he shouldn't torment the child.

There were getting to be more night meetings at church, too, sometimes preachers coming in from the West and sometimes some kind of local meetings Pap said hadn't ought to be held. Sunday was for public worship, he said, and those evening meetings were only good for riling people up. But Biney never wanted to miss a one of them. I didn't care if she and Barbie went to crushes every night of the week when they had young men counted off to take them, but whenever there was a night meeting, Biney was sure to pester me into driving her and Barbie. Her brother Dave was always going somewhere with his girl, and my brother Hen was usually running off to the Gap to be with Annie Keene. Annie's people weren't Mennonite, and he didn't take her to church meetings, though even if they had been, Hen wasn't the sort to spend any extra time in church.

It wasn't exactly my favorite place either, but it was something to do, and when Biney got an idea into her head I hadn't much choice, especially with Mammy shaking her head and saying what a shame it was for the girls not to have a ride. I usually said I didn't see why they couldn't walk the two miles to Paradise, when they didn't have any trouble longshanking it to the post office every day, but Mam would give me a look and say something about what she thought she'd have for dinner the next day or bake come Saturday. Since it was always something I had a special weakness for, I'd shrug my shoulders and get ready to hitch up the buggy after supper, knowing full well I was as likely as not to come home alone in the dark if Barbie and Biney got offered rides with any young men.

Biney fussed as much as usual to get to the mission meeting they were having at the Paradise Church the Thursday after Easter. Pap said the whole mission business sounded to him like a lot of meddling. Turning Christian was something personal you decided on your own, he said, not something you forced down people like a bolus down a sick horse. He wondered what foolishness Ike Eby would be up to next. "Now, Pap," Mammy said, "it can't do any harm," and I knew I might as well get ready to hitch Bluebell to the buggy.

Paradise Mennonite was our home church, though they only had services there every other Sunday with Sunday school on afternoons of the off weeks, when we went to Hershey's Church where the graveyard was, to catch the preaching that moved around between those two places and the Old Road Meetinghouse. Paradise wasn't a very big place, but it had four churches, one Presbyterian and one Episcopal and St. John's Evangelical United Brethren all stretched out along the Pike, and ours just south off the Cherry Hill Road. It wasn't a very long hike, and we walked it often enough except Sundays, when Pap drove us over in the two-seated surrey because he said we showed more respect that way. It wasn't exactly respect Mam had in mind, making me drive the girls in the buggy. I guess she thought they were of an age when it was proper to send them off in style.

Barbie and I were ready in time, but, as usual, Biney was late. We waited till Mam said, flighty as that girl was, we might as well take the long way and pick her up at Uncle Elias's. She was still primping when we got there and kept us waiting some more, so that by the time we got to the church they were already singing. Barbie and Biney jumped right down and went in through the women's door, but I had to find an empty spot for Bluebell in the carriage shed, and the singing had ended by the time I could slip into the men's side and look around for my cousin Sam and his brothers Hon and Charl. Sam had been on the lookout for me and moved over to make room, but I barely had time to give him a poke in the ribs and look across the aisle to see which girls were at the meeting when Bishop Eby got up and started to preach.

Bishops are pretty important men in our church, though they're not like what the Catholics have or any of that kind of heathendom. I hear tell they live like princes and make the people bow down to them, but our bishops are farmers like anyone else. They're the ones chosen out of the ministers of the district to do the marrying and funerals and to give out communion, but they don't preach regular sermons except at spring and fall communion. This meeting wasn't usual church but a special one, and Bishop Isaac Eby wasn't the sort to miss a trick when it came to putting over another of his projects.

The bee in his bonnet this time was to start up a mission movement, and I wasn't surprised to see who the other men were, sitting on the platform behind the preachers' stand: John Buckwalter and a couple others, but mostly Elias Groff, the Sunday school superintendent over at Strasburg. He and Bishop Eby were always putting their heads together over some kind of change, like the Sunday schools they'd started up all over the county. South around New Providence and Willow Street and Strasburg, people took to them pretty early, but they'd only got picked up in Paradise and Hershey's when I was six or seven.

Pap didn't approve of Sunday schools, and he didn't approve of Bishop Eby, even if they were first cousins and Bishop Eby just about five years older than he was. Pap said it must have meant something that Ike Eby was born the year of the School Act when they made everyone go to school in English. It had been nothing but fuss, Pap said, from the time he got the lot maybe twenty years back and was chosen minister.

Pap said his daddy never got over how out of a class of sixteen men the Bible with the lot in it fell to the only one who couldn't talk German and had to do all his preaching in English, and it only got worse when he was chosen bishop. Pap always said his granddaddy who was the great bishop wouldn't have stood for such nonsense. But then Pap grew up talking German a lot cleaner than you hear much in the county nowadays, though we didn't use it at home any more after my oldest brothers, Enos and Bob, married English wives so it wasn't polite. I never learned to talk it right, so I didn't mind that Bishop Eby preached in English. In fact, that might have been one reason he was so popular.

Isaac Eby wasn't as tall as I was, but he was a good-sized man, thick and deep with a square face that turned red when he talked, though his cheeks were red all the time— from ploughing the wrong fields at the wrong time, Pap said—and his nose was fleshy with sort of a knob at the end, not slender and half-arched like Pap's from the Hershey side.

The bishop always started kind of slow, but soon his face was red and he was leaning out at us while he talked. His subject was "Feed My Lambs" and he told us how anyone who followed Christ had an obligation to bring others into the fold and went on to talk about how people all around us needed help and we weren't giving them any. He talked about the poor people in the city and about the closer ones in the hills that had to hire out on farms to earn bread but never got the kind they needed. We had to feed their souls, he said, and then he talked about some of the good work starting to come out of the Paradise Church and said we should pray for more people like Mary Denlinger who'd gone off last year to work at the Home Mission in Chicago. But we should remember the people needing help close to home, too, he said.

Bishop Eby was a good speaker, but I wasn't particularly interested in turning missionary, and I was fifteen, when it was easy to stop listening. John Mellinger was sitting at the end of the bench, so interested I thought his ears would bend forward, and I couldn't see past him very well to the women's side. What I could get a view of besides the preachers' platform were the benches facing it on either side where the old people sat so they'd be close enough to hear.

While Bishop Eby kept on talking I looked them over and found myself counting how many there were: nine on the women's side and just four on the men's, though the other benches were pretty much full of younger people. The old women all had caps on over their hair. Older women put them on when they got dressed up, just like Mam did. A couple of them were pretty fancy, too, but the women weren't dressed any special way except that most of them had capes over their shoulders with the front points tucked under at the waist. I knew all of them, of course, and couldn't see as they looked particularly interested in what the bishop was saying, or the men either. In fact most of the men, especially, looked as if they'd been carved out of wood. I knew they'd come there to find out what was going on, not to help the bishop set up more newfangledness. Mostly I couldn't help watching old Peter Eby. The whole time the bishop was talking, I never saw him twitch a muscle.

He was as old-fashioned as they came, and I knew he wasn't one for changes and mission meetings and such. He never could abide Ike Eby and his English preaching. Peter Eby was in his seventies, almost ten years older than the bishop. He was Ike Eby's first cousin, too, just like he was Pap's and named like Pap for their grandfather Bishop Peter Eby. We saw a fair bit of him because my oldest sister Sarah had married his son. Besides, my pap always liked him. But he had a reputation round about, and most people called him Peter the Hermit because they said he got funny after his three youngest daughters married men who couldn't talk German (what we younger ones called Dutch). My sister Sarah could talk it though, and I guess old Peter Eby was as close to our family as he was to anyone. I was surprised even to see him at an English meeting, but I guess he'd heard that Bishop Eby was up to something and wanted to find out about it for himself.

By now the bishop was telling us we had to reach out and do as much as the heathen Samaritan but if we were real Christians, we had to feed the hungry with the bread of life. Then all of a sudden he said, "Let us pray."

There was a shuffle while everybody stood up and turned around and knelt against the benches. Bishop Eby always did that to us, catching us off guard. As soon as we were down and the grown-ups had their faces hidden, Sam and I put our heads together and started to whisper behind our arms while the bishop prayed. Sam said in my ear that Charl had been tickling suckers under the creek bank and putting them in the watering trough. Uncle Menno didn't know right away why the horses shied and wouldn't drink, but he was plenty mad when he found out. The two of us started to laugh at that, till we had to stuff our arms in our mouths so no one would notice besides Charl and Hon. They were eleven and nine and not likely to snitch on us, but we hadn't counted on John Mellinger on the other side. He gave Sam a nudge with his elbow, and I knew we'd better straighten out or there'd be the dickens to pay. The Mellingers were pretty churchy, and they were all more or less related and likely to tell Pap. He didn't hold by mission meetings, but he had clear ideas about what was proper for church.

But it was easier to whisper than to listen to the prayer, because the whispering helped you forget how much your knees hurt against the floor. Mammy had big spots on hers like bruises that never went away. Housemaid's knee, she called it, though Pap said it was the flesh warring against the spirit and the church should think of getting rugs. I forgot the prayer and was thinking about Mammy's knees, wondering if mine would get like that if the prayer went on much longer, when Bishop Eby said "Amen" and everyone stood up, turned around, and sat down, us younger ones moving late and fast, as though we'd been listening and knew the prayer was over the same time as everybody else.

Bishop Eby sat down then, and the other men on the platform got up one by one and talked some, Elias Groff and the others all saying how important it was to carry on our duty and how lazy the church had been for so long. The very least we could do was take the Word to places like the Welsh Mountains where we had the heathen among us, he said.

While he and the others talked I couldn't help paying some attention, it sounded so exciting—like a kind of adventure. When I thought to look around, I saw that most other people must have thought so too, all so quiet and interested you could have heard a pin drop.

As for John Mellinger sitting at the end of the bench, I wasn't sure he wasn't ready to sprout wings and fly to heaven through the church roof, if it hadn't been a bit undignified for the way people behaved in our church. When the bishop got up again and asked people what they wanted to do, he was the first to stand up and say we'd be failing in our Christian duty if we didn't preach the Gospel, though he added that it might help some of us closer to home, too, who could use a stronger dose of what the Bible says. At that Sam looked over and rolled the corners of his mouth down at me, and I winked back, because we both knew John Mellinger had people like us in mind and our paps, who weren't all fired up over missions and Sunday schools and changes, or afraid to chew tobacco or take a nip now and then if they felt like it. Pap said the church was changing into a nest of wild men, and old Peter Eby said something stronger, that it had turned *schwärmerisch.*

I couldn't help looking at him while Bishop Eby said we were all agreed, then, and he hoped we'd all support the Lancaster County Sunday School Mission. By now the bishop's face looked like a piece of red flannel, and if he wasn't exactly smiling, you could tell he was wearing a great big grin inside. But not old Peter Eby. You couldn't say he was pale except beside the bishop, but his face could have been set in concrete. He'd sat like a statue through all the talk and never batted an eye till after Milt Denlinger stood up and gave the pitch for the singing. Then while everybody was being carried along by the music, old Eby stood up, turned his back to the bishop and the others in the preachers' box, and walked the length of the church and out the men's door. I nudged Sam, and we both watched him as far as we could see without turning our heads.

As soon as the meeting was over and we got outside, Sam whistled and said Peter the Hermit sure had a way of letting everyone know where he stood on things. We both laughed a bit, wondering what Ike Eby thought of his cousin's contrariness, but from what I could see, he wasn't bothered any. The bishop was standing near the door talking with some of the other men about the mission society. I was glad he was too busy to come over and talk to us like he did sometimes, making me feel a hundred miles tall and asking if we ever went over to St. John's and whether we thought the United Brethren services were exciting, that so many young people went to them evenings. But the bishop had other things on his mind tonight, and Sam and I had a chance to slip past the grown-ups and look across to where the girls were.

They were bunched like flowers beside the picket fence, most of them wearing short coats or sweaters against the night air. I remember Lillie in a maroon dress, sort of velvety with ribbons on it. She didn't pay me much attention till years later, so I winked at Annie Ressler and smiled across at Lena Hostetter. I was too young to court, you know, but Sam and I were priming, and I couldn't go home till I got the tip from Barbie and Biney anyway. Little by little we moved closer together until the young men were beside the girls they were interested in while Sam and I hung back a bit, being too young to do more than wink and call over things we thought were smart if we saw the chance.

Biney was next to a new young man I half recognized from over at Mellinger's Church, Amos Landis, and she was smiling and chattering to beat the band. He had his hands behind his back and kept staring down to where he was moving his feet as though he was studying out a little dance. Biney liked special meetings because people came to them from churches all around, not just Hershey's and Paradise. It opened things up, she said, and gave her room to look around so she didn't have to settle for leavings.

It didn't take me long to see that Enos Barge was there, too, and had moved right over to Barbie. His home church was Strasburg, but he'd turned up at a lot of services at Paradise the last year, I thought. He was about the height of the bishop, shorter than me but a lot thicker, being full grown (and well grown at that), with a good chest on him and a serious face with brows like a heavy line drawn over his eyes. His mouth wasn't thin, but it was serious too, like

19 ◊

a line drawn on the bottom of his face to match the one on the top. I couldn't tell what he was saying to Barbie, but he was standing close and talking fast while she hung her head and gave out an answer now and then. I dawdled and hung around for all of ten minutes, waiting to find out what was going on. Finally I walked up to them and said to Barb, "Do you want a ride home or don't you?" "Oh, there you are, Silas," Barbie said, all pink and flustered. Enos looked at me and at Barbie. Then he said, "You might as well go on home. I'll look to her."

Barbie may have said something, thinking to stop me, but I wasn't about to wait around longer and find out. I could see that Biney was in shape to get herself home, too, so I gave a call to Sam and hightailed it for the carriage shed, Charl and Hon right at our heels, looking to get a ride as far as the Strasburg Road and save some shoe leather on the walk home.

III.

Pap didn't say much about it, but I knew he wasn't any more pleased than Mam that my brother Hen was keeping company with Annie Keene. It wasn't that Pap was conservative like, say, old Peter Eby, but he had convictions, and he and Mam both hoped us kids would join church eventually, the same way they had. Joining church was different in those days, something you did when you were grown-up and sure you'd decided for certain, usually after you'd been married a year or so and settled. Then you got baptized and promised to live by the church till you died. That way young people had a chance to get the wildness out of their systems and be serious about what they decided, not carried away one day by something they were sorry for the next.

Our church didn't hold much with people getting carried away, and Pap didn't hold with trying to force people into turning Mennonite. We had to come to it on our own, he said, because no one could make a decision that serious for anyone else, but if we were brought up right, chances were we'd all join same as Pap and all his brothers and sisters had and my brothers Enos and Bob and my sister Sarah.

Mammy always went along with what Pap did, but she was more worried over Hen than he was, probably because she'd already lost a daughter by Lizzie marrying Harry Hess. She always looked embarrassed for half a second when people asked how Harry and Lizzie were making out in Atlantic City, as if she still didn't really believe she had a daughter so worldly, and she always gave a funny look to the fancy boxes they brought us at Christmas before she'd start to open them. I knew she was afraid she'd lose Hen the way she had Lizzie but maybe worse. Lizzie's man at least was from Mennonite stock, but Annie Keene didn't have a drop of Mennonite blood. Her pap farmed on shares over in Puddingtown near the Gap, and if they went to church at all, it sure wasn't to a Mennonite one.

I'd only seen Annie a couple times, once when they auctioned off the Kreider place and once over at Marsh's store in the Gap. She was big and ruddy and wearing a dress with bright flowers, her arms bare and a good patch of her neck showing around a ruffle. The flowers were orange and picked up the color of the hair all fluffed around her face. She was laughing both times, with her mouth red and her cheeks pink. I guess I gawked some when I saw her at the store, because she caught me out and said, "What's the matter, sonny? Never seen a woman before?" Anyone could see that Annie wasn't the kind of girl Mennonite boys married if they were thinking about joining the church. When Hen and Annie had the fight and broke up, some of the family were pretty relieved.

We didn't find out about it till after breakfast the next morning, though Hen was grumpier than usual when he got up, and I remembered that he'd stomped up the stairs and thrown down his shoes like he wanted them to drop through the floor into the spare room when he got in the night before, then got into bed and yanked the covers half off me. I sat up and said, "For cripe's sake, Hen," but he rolled his back to me and didn't say more than he said when he got up and stomped to the barn to start the milking. At breakfast he kept his head bent over his plate until he shoved back his chair and stomped out again, slamming the kitchen door. The rest of us looked at each other, because after breakfast we always had devotions and prayer. "What's got into that boy now?" Mammy said, and Pap looked back across the table to her. "I don't know, Mother, but we might as well leave him be." I smiled to myself, because Hen was grown and always did what he wanted anyway.

The rest of us went into the front room then, and Pap picked up the big English Bible from the table and sat down with it in his Morris chair. Barb and I plunked onto the fancy green chairs, and Mam and Martha arranged themselves on the wood settee with the buffalo robe on it to make it softer, while Pap opened the Bible and read.

We had a German Bible, too, with fancy writing in red and black between the Testaments and a leather cover, but it was in the parlor next door that only got used for company, and Pap always read from the English one. I always figured he could read German, though I never really knew, because he was born after the School Act and had gone to English schools. He and Mam could rattle away in Dutch to each other and had talked it all the time when the older kids were little, I knew. My sister Sarah and her family hardly talked anything else, and her husband John was the only one who read the Bible on the parlor table when they came to visit. Pap always read to us from the English one before we got down on our knees and covered our faces against the chairs until he said "Amen" and we could get up again and go on about our work.

Then Pap and I took down our jackets from the pegs beside the kitchen door, and I followed him out to the barn while Mammy and the girls clattered dishes behind us and Barbie sang the way she always did when she went about her chores. The song was silly, I guess, half a nursery rhyme and half a kind of hymn. I remember it because Barbie sang it a lot. Later I got Martha to copy it off for me. The tune was "Twinkle, Twinkle Little Star," but it went on. Whenever I think about it, I remember Barbie's voice singing it:

> When the glorious sun is set,
>> When the grass with dew is wet,
> Then you show your little light.
>> Twinkle, twinkle all the night.

In the last verse she asks the star who made it shine like that, and the star says God did. But Pap and I were out of earshot by the time she got that far, and coming on Hen, grumpy as a bear, was enough to chase music out of anyone's head.

He'd turned the steers into the barnyard and was pitching dung out one of the stable doors. Pap muttered under his breath that at least Henry was doing something appropriate. I started to laugh, but Pap gave me a look that shut me up again and told me to fetch a pitchfork and see if I could keep up. I followed him through another of the doors under the overhang to where the pitchforks were propped at the back and then dragged on through the barn to the steer pen while Pap went on to look over the horses and see if the roan was still off his feed.

Being built into a hill, the barn was always dark down there except for the light that came in when some of the doors in the row under the overhang were open, and I liked the dark and the warm animal smells after the bright morning cold. I stood for a minute tamping the pitchfork handle against the floor and listening to the horses stamping like noisy shadows, and Pap saying "So, so" to quiet them so he could check them over, and the grinding sound that meant the roan had gone back to nuzzle a cob and finish off its breakfast.

In the box where we kept the steers Hen was swooping on the litter like he had some personal grudge and wanted it to hurt when he pitched it out the door. He paused now and then to give the bottom half of the door a kick when it tried to swing shut on him, looking black against the morning light. I wasn't anxious to go in there and stood a bit fiddling with the fork till he looked up. "You can help me, damn it," Hen said, and I scuttled to open the inside gate and get busy.

The steer stable always stank to high heaven and half *greisled* me, though Pap said no sane man ever gagged over gold. He wouldn't have raised steers except for the manure. It was what made the tobacco grow, he said, and tobacco was what paid his pap so he could set his sons up on farms and what we had to count on to set us up, too. He'd kept this batch of steers longer than usual, watching the market to see if the depression would lift so he'd get his money out of them and grumbling the while that McKinley knew how to run up a debt but not how to help the farmers.

Low prices or not, I couldn't wait for him to sell off this lot and buy new ones we could put in the meadow for the summer. Working in that stink, it wasn't long till I felt as mad as Hen and hated the things when they turned their white faces to look in at what we were doing. I guess Hen's mood must have been catching, though I felt better when Pap came over with the shovel to help finish off and told me to scoot up the ladder and throw some straw from the mow for fresh bedding. It wasn't quite a ladder, and it was too steep for steps, but I scooted up fast enough, glad to get out of that steer stable.

I didn't hurry getting down, either, so that till I got back, the pen was finished and Hen was leaning against one side of it with his face cradled against his arm. Pap was standing with his arms folded and his hands tucked under his elbows, the way he put them when he was worried over something, like he got them out of the way by instinct when he couldn't use them to fix things up.

"She told me to get out," Hen was saying, "just up and threw me out." Pap had his head bent, listening. I don't think either one noticed I was there, and it didn't strike me as a time to announce myself. I guess Pap was waiting to see what else Hen had to say. Finally he lifted his chin maybe an inch. "Wasn't there some reason?" Pap asked.

It was like Hen twitched. He took a big breath before he said, "We had a fight." Pap made a sound like a cross between an oh and a sigh, and Hen hunched against the rail. Then he threw up his head. "I asked her if she was stepping out on me, if you must know, and she said that was just the sort of thing she'd expect me to ask, coming from a high and mighty Mennonite family." Pap had lowered his chin again, and he made another sound, a real sigh this time.

"She said I'd never trust her, and she should have known better than to get mixed up with me, " Hen went on. "I told her she was being a damned hypocrite and it was how many of my kind she was stepping out with that bothered me. That's when she slapped me. I was so mad I felt like knocking her across the room, but instead I came on home." After a minute he said, "It's over, I guess. I just got to get used to it."

"I guess so," Pap said so quiet you couldn't tell if he was sympathizing with Hen or thinking that maybe now he'd go out with someone respectable. I felt like speaking up and saying good riddance, but Hen started talking again. "If only I could get out of here," he said, and it sounded like he was choking. "Pap, the farm is getting me down. Maybe I should have gone along with Mart last month. He's seeing something, anyway. When we put him on the train and it started pulling out, moving west, I thought I couldn't stand it. I'd have gone along with him just to get out, except—"

"I know," Pap said, quiet as I ever heard him.

"One of us should be home," Hen said like he was pleading. "With Silas still in school we couldn't both go."

"I know, son, I know," Pap said again, tucking his hands deeper under his arms. Hen was still leaning against the rail, staring towards the open door. A couple steers were bunched against the barnyard fence near the pigsty, but it was as though Hen was looking out past them, the whole way across the valley to where the far ridge stretched across the south. Then he shook himself the way he did when he threw water over his face first thing in the morning. "I better hitch up the mules," he said, but he walked to the door and stood staring out a bit longer before he finally turned away and headed towards the horses.

Pap noticed me then. "You better fill the woodbox and get on to school," he said. I realized he'd been staring out at the ridge, too.

When I hauled the wood in from the woodshed, Mam and the girls had carried up the old milk from the stone vault at the end of the cellar and were working over it in the washhouse. Mammy was cutting off the cream, saying the while that she hoped the milk wasn't grassy this time or Mr. Esbenshade at the Paradise store would stop taking her butter. Barbie had the churn ready, and Martha was looking on. "We're low on kindling, too, Silas," Martha said. I thought to myself that she could fetch it as well as I could, but I only said, "You needn't be so bossy," and went out again to fetch an armload of cobs from the shed beside the privy.

Barbie was turning the handle on the churn when I came back through the washhouse. She looked especially pretty when she worked like that, her cheeks bright and her eyes dark and sparkling. Her hair was sort of wispy around her face from having it cut the winter before when she and Martha both had eczema, but it looked pretty from the front with a fringe above her eyes that made her face look round as a baby's. She'd pushed her sleeves up above her elbows so she could work better, but even without seeing how round and full her arm was, you knew she'd make someone the kind of wife Pap always bragged that he'd got.

In the kitchen Mam and Martha were putting on their sunbonnets to tend the chickens and work in the garden. I dumped the cobs in the kindling section of the woodbox and said, "I know why Hen's so grumpy." Then I stood by the range to watch what they'd do.

"You shouldn't tattle, Silas," Mammy said, pulling on her sweater, but Martha stopped tying her bonnet strings and said, "How come?"

"Mammy, do I have to go to school today?"

"You might as well tell us, Silas, instead of teasing the morning away," Mam said, so I knew she wanted to hear and was just pretending not to be interested.

"I wasn't sure you wanted to know," I said. "Guess I better get ready for school."

"Sike!" Martha screeched. "Now you just tell!" I grinned while she ran on about how contrary I was and how I must take after old Grandmother because the Hersheys were never like that. I always did know how to get a rise out of Martha.

"Silas, we got work to do," Mammy said. "Tell it or not, as you please."

I looked at Mam and said, "Hen had a fight with Annie Keene last night." Mam looked half stunned, but Martha gave a chortle and ran to the washhouse door, calling to Barbie that Hen had broken up with that girl. Mam sank down in a rocker and asked me how I knew, and I told her how Hen told Pap in the barn. Barb and Martha were both right there asking questions till Mam hushed them. "We'd best not say anything more about it," she said. "Let Henry tell us himself. And Silas, don't you go talking about it to Sam on the way to school. Hen's private business is his own till he wants us to know it."

By the end of the week all the aunts and uncles and cousins did know, but by then Pap had driven Hen over to the railroad station at Leaman Place and set him on the twelve o'clock special for a visit with my sister Lizzie and her family at the seashore.

IV.

Our farm had been new when Pap and Mammy moved into it, but now that the trees had filled up around it and they'd lived in it more than thirty years, it was comfortable—and still more modern than the houses Uncle Menno and Uncle Elias lived in, though Mam said she'd have settled for the home place where she and Pap farmed when they got married until Granddad Hershey got George Beiler, the Amish contractor, to build ours. It fronted on the Strasburg Road and ran back along the road between Blackhorse and Paradise with a couple bites out, on the corner where the hotel was and further back where Beiler had kept out some places to burn lime.

I thought our place looked trim and handsome. It sat back a piece on a little rise that fell again beyond the buildings, rolled down across the fields, and finally settled into the meadow on the north end of the property just before the Strasburg Railroad tracks. The lane ran up straight between the house and the barn, both red but the house brick with the doors and windows marked out in white, like the balcony white above the east end and the fence I had to whitewash every spring that marked the yard off from the lane and the fields on two sides and the orchard behind.

Except for the stone base, the barn was red, too, like the stable doors framed in white to match the house in a neat row under the overhang. Even the pigsty in the corner of the barnyard nearest the house was red. From the road you hardly saw the red tobacco shed tall behind the barn or the other outbuildings.

My brother Enos's grandson has the farm now. It doesn't look much different than it used to, but he knocked out the stone vault at the end of the cellar, and I doubt that the house will stand much longer with the foundation gone.

Still, it was a good place to live, and good country for farming tobacco. We were less than three miles from the east end of Strasburg where the brick tobacco warehouse stood at the end of the railroad tracks, so big you'd think it could have held all the tobacco in the county, except that there was another past the square and still another just north in Paradise not far from the church, all of them full and not buying much because of the depression. There was another in the Gap, down the Strasburg Road in the other direction.

But I always thought the best thing about our place was having family all around, my brother Enos down the road and three Hershey uncles less than a mile away where my Granddad Hershey settled them before he died. We didn't see much of Uncle John, Pap's oldest brother that lived on the farm my granddad had split off from the home place, because he and Pap's two oldest sisters had all married Mellingers—two brothers and a sister. Being churchy and related half a dozen ways, they visited mostly with each other. All their kids were grown-up and married anyway, so it wasn't much fun to go to those places. We didn't see much of Mammy's people, either, the Buckwalters and Neffs and Kreiders from down close to Lancaster. When I asked Pap once how he came to marry a wife from down that way, he smiled and said a good woman was worth going after.

Mostly, I liked having Uncle Elias and Uncle Menno so close, Uncle Menno especially, just a mile towards the Gap in a big old stone house back a lane you turned into between stone posts before the Belmont Road. It even had a name, Round Top Farm.

That house must have had fifteen rooms, most of them with fireplaces, but all of them were bricked up and they'd put in iron stoves like ours, though Uncle Elias said nothing would keep the front rooms warm because the house faced north. You could tell it was English built, he said, because no Dutchman would be so dumb. But, then, they mostly lived in the kitchen in the back anyway, like everyone else, where it was comfortable enough, what with my cousins Bess and Sam and Charl and Hon, not to mention Uncle Menno studying the newspaper, and Aunt Mary singing while she puttered around the range, and Aunt Sue, my old maid aunt, rocking somewhere and aiming her ear trumpet at you when she wanted to hear what was going on.

Uncle Menno was four years older than Pap, but he'd been a bachelor till he was past thirty, so his kids weren't far from my age. Bess was oldest, the same age as Barbie. She and Barb and Martha got on all right, but they weren't close like Barb and Biney or like Sam and me.

Sam was eleven days older than me. Looking back, it seems like we were always together. We'd sat together in school from the time we started, unless the teacher separated us for making too much ruckus. School laws weren't so fussy then, and I knew people who quit after fifth grade, which is why Sam and I were both mad that we had to keep on after we turned fifteen and finish out the year—and the school, as far as it went.

It was my brother Hen who'd talked both our paps into making us finish out the year, with what he said about how important it was to be educated. He'd gone to school as far as it went and always had his nose in a book when he wasn't running with Annie Keene. Hen was a nuisance, we agreed. Sam said he might as well be brother to him, too, the way he ran both our lives.

Still, we both always wanted to know whatever Hen was up to, and I knew Sam and his folks would be as interested as I was when we got the postcard from Atlantic City where Hen was visiting at Lizzie's. So, soon as supper was over and the women were washing up, I headed down the road to show it to them. When I got in the kitchen Bess and the boys crowded right around to see it, and Aunt Mary dried her hands from where she was washing dishes and sat down beside Uncle Menno to get a look at it, while Aunt Sue said, "What's that? What's the boy got?" till Uncle Menno shouted to her it was a card from Hen, and she came over to see it too.

Hen didn't say much on the back, only that Lizzie and her man and the kids were all well and the day he'd be back. What we were all interested in was the front, because Harry Hess had printed up a picture of his business as an advertisement. It showed six men leaning against a row of wicker rolling chairs and up above them a big sign: "Hess Rolling Chairs, Fifty Cents an Hour." Most of the men looked sort of scruffy, and one had a cigar in his hand.

On the back, under what Hen said, Lizzie had scrawled, "Can you tell which is Harry?" But there was no problem telling Harry Hess. He was at the end of the line with one hand on a chair and the other on his hip, his mouth straight and sober like he didn't want to look proud, but well as he was doing, he couldn't help it. It showed in the way his eyes looked straight out at you. Martha said his eyes looked hard, but my brother Hen said it was just that Harry Hess looked at things squarely and was thinking all the time. He was a proper-looking man, and Barbie said she knew how Lizzie had come to marry him. All of us studied over that picture, Uncle Menno's family because they never knew what Harry Hess's business looked like before and me because I was proud at having a brother-in-law so important.

"Look how fancy the chairs are," Bess said, "with those fringes on top so it's like they're covered with parasols."

I snorted. "They have to be fancy to fetch fifty cents an hour, I guess, when you can get a good meal in Lancaster for half that, and tobacco only bringing sixty cents a hundred."

"Who are those other men?" Hon asked.

Seems like I never could help showing off a bit about Lizzie. "Pushers," I said. "You don't think someone like Harry Hess runs people up and down the boardwalk himself, do you?"

Me saying that must have riled Charl, or else he was just trying to make himself big by putting me down. He was three years younger than Sam and me and always ready to get himself noticed somehow or other. "I guess someone like Harry Hess wouldn't work if he could get someone else to do it for him," Charl said. Sam and I glared at him, and Uncle Menno said, "Charles, watch your tongue." I was about ready to take my postcard and march on home except that Aunt Sue had picked it up and was studying over it, her eyes being sharper than her ears.

"What's that over to the side?" she asked in the loud voice she used so she could hear herself. "What's that head doing there?" We all bent to look where she was pointing, and sure enough, if you looked real close you could see the outline of a head over to one side behind the man with the cigar. "Palmistry and Phrenology," Hon said, sounding out the syllables. I saw he was reading some fine print from the side of the stall next to Harry Hess's. "Why, that's a fortune teller," Aunt Sue said. "Harry must be right next to a fortune teller's stand!"

I felt my neck getting red, and everybody was quiet for a minute. I know now that the grown-ups were all tender at what got said about Lizzie. Nobody but Aunt Sue would have said that in front of me, but she was half queer in the head from nursing my grandmother till they got Mrs. Divet to do it and she moved in with Uncle Menno. Embarrassed as everybody else was, she didn't even notice but looked up real perky and said with a big smile, "I got my fortune told once!"

"Tell us about it another time," Aunt Mary shouted at her, scooping up the postcard and handing it back to me. Then she asked if I could eat a piece of pie left from supper, and Uncle Menno asked what my pap thought about the Populist agitators in the West, Hon hanging right beside him at any talk to do with politics even when he was nine.

I didn't stay long after the pie, and Sam grabbed his jacket to walk me part way home, knowing I was still part miffed from Charl and Aunt Sue. Neither of us said anything till we got past the posts and onto the road. Then Sam said, "I think it's exciting to have a sister at the seashore. Wish I could trade off Bess for Lizzie." We both started to laugh, and I said I'd trade off Martha for just about anybody except that I couldn't imagine many takers.

We walked on a bit, and Sam said, "I sure envy Hen." I asked why, because he was at the seashore or because he'd lost his girl?

"Come on, Sike," Sam said. "You know they'll get back together again as soon as he comes home from Lizzie's.

Anyway, that's what my mam says." I didn't answer because I hadn't thought before of Hen and Annie starting up again. Sam sighed. "It sure must be exciting to go with a girl like that," he said, and I said, "Yeah, I guess so," though I hadn't thought of it before, at least not to say it. We'd got to the hotel by then where Sam turned back, and I went on home in the dusk.

We didn't have to worry about getting the postcard over to Uncle Elias's, because when I got home Biney was in the kitchen and Aunt Annie too. "We got to be getting back," Aunt Annie said. "I told Elias I'd only be a half hour." She didn't move from the rocker, and Mam said, "Show Annie the card, Silas." Biney scuttled to look over her mam's shoulder, pointing and chattering same as usual, but Aunt Annie hardly looked at it, like she hadn't energy to pay the card much attention. She was thinner than Mam and with a pointy nose. Her hair was greyer than Mam's too, with a white streak on either side where it was pulled back to the bun women wore, and her dress hung flat on her chest, not full and round like Mammy's.

She finally got up like she didn't really want to go. "Grandmother will be wanting something and sending Mrs. Divet to pester Elias," she said, "so I guess I better get home."

"Can't we stay just a little longer?" Biney asked, but when Aunt Annie shook her head, saying Biney could stay if she wanted, Biney grabbed her sweater so her mam wouldn't have to walk home alone. Barb put hers on too, to walk them out the lane. After dark the women generally went the long way by the road instead of taking the shortcut across the meadow. Even so, Mam called after them to look out for tramps before she shut the door and sank into the rocker Aunt Annie had left.

"I don't know how that woman runs a farm," Mammy said. Pap had come in from the front room and was leafing through a catalogue by the kerosene light. Martha was plumping the cushion on the kitchen settee so she could spread out and put up her feet. "Save room for me, Moss," I said mostly to make her mad, but she hardly noticed, listening to Mam and wrinkling her forehead into frown marks over her nose. I don't know how Martha got that nickname, except maybe because she laid around so much, but we called her that half the time, just like I got called Sike. In those days Martha was pretty, her face not so round as Barbie's and her eyes a light clear blue, but so serious Pap said he'd have to find a bishop for her to marry if he wanted to get her off his hands, teasing that she wasn't fast enough when Bishop Eby was widowed ten years back and got snapped up by the Leaman widow.

We all teased Martha, I guess because she asked for it, always fussing over herself, even if I think now it was Mammy's fault for spoiling her after the scarlet fever. Still, well as Martha looked after herself, she was fierce to look after us, too. Nothing was too good for her family, the Hershey side anyhow, and hardly anyone was good enough for us to marry. Aunt Annie had been a Kreider and almost fit for Uncle Elias but not quite as lively as she should be, so right away Martha trained her good ear at what Mam was saying.

"Annie hardly has strength to keep up with her own work," Mammy said, "much less keep an eye on Mrs. Divet and your mother to see that the house doesn't burn down."

Pap kept turning over leaves in the catalogue, deliberately not answering. Grandmother was a sore point between him and Mam, like it was a sore point that Uncle Elias got the home farm after my folks had worked it five years and counted on staying there till Elias got married and took it. Mam never could resist noticing out loud whenever Aunt Annie and Uncle Elias didn't come up to snuff or pointing out what a bad bargain the home farm turned out to be with my grandmother to go with it. "It's not as if your mother couldn't look after herself if she wanted to," Mam said.

"Now Barbara," Pap said, not raising his voice but saying it like he'd been over it a hundred times before. "Mother's a sick woman and has been for years."

"If you say so, Peter," Mam said, the look on her face saying she knew better. Of course Martha thought she did too and spoke right up from where she was resting herself. "If you ask me, all that's wrong with her is being *gross* and *dick*—and contrary like the rest of the Ebys."

"You don't know she's not sick," Pap said, "and don't forget you're part Eby." Martha sniffed and leaned back on the settee. "I still think she's putting on," she said and closed her eyes. I started to laugh, because Martha always got mad over Grandmother. "You sure have lots of Eby in you, Moss," I said, but she kept her eyes shut and pretended not to hear.

"Did you hear what Annie asked me?" Mam said to Pap, half exasperated but with a certain satisfaction as much as to say Aunt Annie and Uncle Elias had done it again.

"Wasn't paying attention," Pap said, pushing the catalogue away. "With Biney in the room there's too much gabble to keep up. What'd she have to say?"

"She wants us to keep an eye on Grandmother for a couple of weeks while she and Elias visit the children."

"Oh," Pap said, drawing it out. Everything was quiet for a minute except for the fire crackling in the range and Mammy's rockers clicking against the floor till she said, "I told Annie all right but it couldn't be till May because of Sarah and the family coming. I didn't know what else I could say," Mammy added, "if Annie and Elias have to go running off in the middle of planting. It would be easy enough if your mother would leave that bed and come to stay over here, but at least this way we won't have to worry about her burning this house down."

Pap nodded. "If it will be a help to Annie and Elias," he said.

Just then Barbie came in, her cheeks pink and her eyes brown and bright. "What are all you so glum over?" she said. "Aunt Annie told me we're going to look after Grandmother. Can I stay over with Biney and help out?"

V.

Spring was coming on fast. I measured it from the colors of the trees when the yellow-green got darker—and from how much wood I had to split and carry into the house. We hardly lit the stove in the front room now (morning devotions were pretty chilly), though I still had to haul in wood and corncobs, especially Mondays for the washing and Saturdays when Mam did the baking.

Pap shaved off the beard he grew winters, too, and one by one the cows came in fresh, and Mam packed away the feather comforters, and the stove pipe through the bedroom floor stopped giving off heat, so it was as cold when we went to bed as it was when we splashed our faces in the morning. Pap's timothy was up, showing lighter green under the young wheat, and the lilacs were blooming in the backyard. It was a good spring. Pap said the tobacco was coming along quicker than usual under the muslin. Fast as it was growing, he was afraid it would turn spindly and sprinkled it with water mixed with dry steer blood he'd saved from butchering, to keep it strong.

My brother Mart wrote from out west that the season was behind where he was in the Dakotas. The snow had only left the fields, and it was still too wet to work them, Mart said, but Mr. Stark that he worked for found enough to keep him and the others busy. Reading that, Mam clicked her tongue. "You'd think that boy would have had sense enough to stay in a decent place," she said. Pap smiled and answered, "Now, Barbara. The boy wanted an adventure, but he'll be back." Somehow almost all the young men who went away did come back, too, after they'd looked around and had a chance to realize how good life was in our valley, especially in spring when they remembered the lilacs and the forsythia and the marsh marigolds flashing bright and golden, while the fields rolled out soft and yellow-green between the ridges.

Mart wrote he'd stick out the season. He'd made friends with a Swedish fellow and wrote that Swen took him along to church. He told me later Swen took him to dances, too, but he didn't say that in his letters, only that church was a lot different. "What's he doing in a Lutheran church?" Mammy said when she read about it. Pap said, "Nothing else around, I guess. We can be thankful he's in church." It strikes me that some ways Pap was more liberal about things like that than Mammy, even if his pap had been a minister and his granddaddy a bishop, and even if he was old-fashioned about changes in the church. "He'll be back," Pap would say, and Mammy would reach over and squeeze his hand, thinking of Lizzie.

But the sure sign of spring was when the outsiders came around, when the tramps started wandering along the roads again after wintering in the poorhouse, knocking on the kitchen door to beg for meals. Mam never turned them away. "You can always spare food," she said, but she kept a set of dishes separate for them, and none of us ever took a drink from the coconut shell at the pump in the yard. Mammy said she wondered if they didn't somehow mark her place, as often as they came round, and Pap chuckled, saying people like that could always spot a softhearted woman.

Gypsies came, too. Mam was half afraid of them and said they'd have to see Pap when they knocked at the door and asked if they could camp in the meadow. When they found him, he always said they could, but I could tell he wasn't happy about it. He generally cleared his throat and said, "If you're in my meadow, I trust my wife's chickens will be safe." He'd get a grin back while he stood with his hands tucked under his arms and they thanked him, the men dark and oily-looking and the women standing back in their bright skirts, usually with one or two little kids peeking out from behind them.

We were happy when the Peddlar Woman came by, trudging up the lane with her cases loaded on her back. "How goes it with you this year, Mrs. Hershey?" she'd call, and Mammy would throw open the kitchen door and take the packs off her shoulder and settle them onto the table. Pap said the Peddlar Woman was half gypsy, but she didn't dress like one. She always wore sober clothes that looked dusty and a pair of men's workboots, but she half talked like one, or that's what it sounded like to me. You could understand her well enough. It's just that the sentences went together different, and her words sounded sort of creaky, like they hadn't been greased in the right places. Listening to her talking to Mammy and telling what she had special this time always made me imagine she'd come to our lane from the other end of the world, even if I knew she'd just walked from the Rancks' and the Witmers' and from Uncle Menno's before that.

It must have been that spring I got the bow tie, and I remember Barbie admiring some calico the same time. "Sure would make a pretty quilt," she said, fingering some sprigged pink stuff, then some in yellow. Usually Mam and the girls pieced quilts out of dress scraps and what was left over from other things, but girls Barbie's age generally wanted at least one fancy one with all bought material.

The Peddlar Woman smiled over at Mammy like she knew a secret. "Must be a young man and a wedding soon in the family, no, Mrs. Hershey?"

"No!" Barbie said, and she said it so cross that we all stared. Barbie's face got red and she looked around at us with an expression half-surprised and half-embarrassed. Then she looked down again at the material her hand was still on and said real low, "I ain't planning any wedding."

I don't think Barb really wanted that calico, but she said she'd take it and went to fetch her butter money from upstairs. The Peddlar Woman said, "So sorry I am, Mrs. Hershey," but Mam nodded that it was all right and said something about trouble with her young man. "You know how young people are," Mam said.

Except for the gypsies, the only people Mam hated to see come round were the beggars from the Welsh Mountains, shriveled black women driving wagons we never thought would make it back out the lane, as rickety as they looked and as tired and skinny as the horses were, always walking like they were too old and weak to pull their own tails, much less those wagons.

Since my sister Sarah and her family had moved to Weaverland, they were a lot closer to the mountains than we were. Sarah said no one left meat hanging in the smokehouse near where they lived. She had guinea hens, too, and when I asked why she kept such cackly things, she said they were the peaceful way to guard the henhouse.

Her husband John said they needed them to look for buzzards, and I knew he meant the one family in the mountains that had a name.

The Welsh Mountains were north of us and to the east. When we drove up to Sarah's I couldn't help staring at them off to the right like a shadow rising out of the farmlands and spreading on till we got past New Holland. They always half scared me, and all of us were nervous when the black people from the mountains came by. "Now they've looked us over, we'd better look to the brooder house," Mam said, watching the old horse dragging down the lane, the wagon heavier now by a bag of snitz or corn meal she'd sent Barbie to fetch from the flour room while she stayed at the door. Still, when I thought back on the sermon Bishop Eby gave the night he and Elias Groff started the mission society, I could see why they figured the Welsh Mountains was just the place to need spiritual feeding, even if I had trouble thinking of those black people as lambs.

We heard at church the bishop was sending a delegation to the mountains to look over the situation and bring back a report, but we didn't hear how it came out till Biney came scooting down the hill one day while I was splitting wood and Barbie was pulling plants to set out in the garden from the coldframe beside the woodshed.

"I got to tell you what Jake Ressler said!" Biney called, her mouth going faster than her feet even before she came up to us. Barb stood up and wiped her hands on her apron. It never took much for me to put down the axe, so I went over too.

Biney talked so much your forgot how sharp she was under that flightiness, but when she wasn't setting up parties and meetings and young men, she could be worth listening to. She wasn't soft and pretty like Barb but wiry, and with so much energy it was like she had to let it out by running and talking and setting up plans so she wouldn't burst from it. She didn't get it from her pap or mam, but she was always going. I guess that's why she and Barb got on, because neither one of them ever walked if they could run.

"Jake Ressler stopped by," she said, still huffing from running across the meadow. "He and the bishop and a couple others went to the mountain yesterday!" Barbie and I both grinned because it was fun to see Biney full of something.

"Nothing in that," I said. "We all knew they were going."

"Silas!" Barbie said, sounding like Martha but smiling and not meaning it the bossy way Martha did.

"You can chop wood as easy as you can listen," Biney said, cocking her head at me. Being outnumbered, I shut up. "He said they went over to some shanties near the Blue Rocks," Biney said. Barbie and I both paid attention at that, because everyone knew the Blue Rocks was the worst spot in the Welsh Mountains. People said there was a cave near there, and what was missing in the valley you could find in the hill.

"They tried a couple shanties," Biney went on, "and no one opened up, so they went on, moving from one place to another till they came to one even worse than the others, all ramshackle and thrown together, you know, and with chinks so they could see someone was sitting inside. They knocked, and when no one answered, Bishop Eby pushed open the door."

Biney stopped, her hands on her hips and her head on one side, waiting for us to ask her more. Barbie and I just waited.

"Well," Biney said, "can you imagine, they saw an old man, his beard all white and his hair all kinky and silver-looking, and he didn't say a word, just stared off like

45 ◇

he didn't even see them but was looking somewhere beyond, and them all standing there looking at him."

She waited again for Barbie and me to say something. I was too interested, but Barbie told her to get on, and Biney told us the old man didn't talk at first, but then, making his words soft and slurred so they could hardly understand him, he said, "I come here a long time ago because I wanted to be free, and I'm still waitin'."

Bishop Eby knelt down and prayed beside him, Biney said, that old man still staring out like he didn't see any of them with him. When they left, the bishop said it was a sign from the Lord, and they had to start a mission in the mountains.

They got it started, too. It must have been the right thing to do, because none of the teachers or missionaries got murdered there till almost thirty years later. Of course lots of people muttered and grumbled, and old Peter Eby said he didn't know what the church was coming to when it didn't have anything better to do than mind other people's business. But most people reached into their pockets and left something on the table in front of the preachers' platform after church, especially the Mellingers but even my pap and Uncle Elias, so the missions got a good start, good enough that they opened another one in Lancaster a year or so later.

But all that took some time, and while Bishop Eby was busy setting up his missions, we were readying the fields to get the crops in, ploughing and harrowing and rolling them over and over to get out the lumps. In the second week of May Hen came home from the seashore, carrying his bag like he was tired even after two weeks at the ocean. I remember Barbie dashing out to welcome him and Pap telling him he was in time to help take the muslin off the tobacco beds and put in the corn.

VI.

Hen settled in pretty well. He got out the mules and harrowed all right, but he was even more quiet than usual. I couldn't get him to talk even when we went to bed. It was like he was thinking especially hard, but Hen always had done that. At least he sat with the rest of us for morning devotions, and I knew Mammy was relieved as if she'd gotten him back after a longer trip than to the seashore. That May she seemed to bustle around more than ever, not just because Hen was home, but because she was looking forward to my sister Sarah and her family coming down from Weaverland for a visit.

I know myself now that the first of the brood is generally special. There's no doubt that Sarah always was in our family, and with Mammy in particular. Sarah was past thirty then and already had six kids, but she was still pretty, her hair almost black and her eyes bright blue like Martha's. She was trim, too, all but the little belly rounded under her apron so you never could tell when she had another one in the oven. She and John must have made a handsome pair in their courting days, because he was a good-looking man, and Pap said he'd been a high-stepper, with flashy clothes and the fanciest horse around. In those days he'd even had a mustache, so you knew he'd been kicking hard against the traces.

When Pap told me that, I thought at first he was making it up for one of his jokes, but Pap said it was true, only John Eby changed after he married Sarah, so that as long as I remembered, he was stricter than his daddy, old Peter the Hermit. When he converted, he did it all the way, Pap said, taking Sarah and driving up all the way above New Holland so Jonas Martin could baptize them in German. "Das English ist kein Sprache," John Eby said, and he didn't think any more of Bishop Eby's English preaching than his daddy did. His being so conservative was the reason he'd moved them to Weaverland. After they got married, they'd farmed his pap's place near the Gap till about five years back, when he said he'd had enough of English preaching and Sunday schools.

That was before the ruckus in the Weaverland Church, when the progressive ones tried to bring in a pulpit and get rid of the old-fashioned singing table they still used up there. It all ended in Bishop Martin being thrown out of church at fall conference and the people as conservative as he was splitting off to follow him, John Eby at the head of the pack. He and Sarah still went to the same church as before, only now the regular church used it every other Sunday and the Jonas Martin people had it in between.

That meant Mam had to calculate an invitation to Sarah pretty carefully, because it had to be on one of their off Sundays, and it had to be when Ike Eby wasn't around and Jacob Hershey was preaching. He was first cousin once removed to my pap through their daddies and the only one in our district who still did all his preaching in German. But he was almost eighty and didn't preach regularly any more, so when Mam found out he'd be at Hershey's on one of Jonas Martin's off weeks, the letters flew pretty fast to arrange for Sarah and John to come for a visit.

What a time we had waiting for them. Barbie never went off to any crushes those Saturday nights and was worse than Mammy, scuttling around the kitchen to see if everything was ready and then out the door to look if they were in sight yet, till Pap asked if she was expecting the Prince of Wales instead of John and Sarah. But as soon as we heard their carriage clattering down the lane, he was out as fast as the rest of us, ready to lift the kids out of the carriage and shake hands with John while Mam and the girls hugged Sarah and fussed over the children and Hen shook hands, hanging back a bit. Till we got the carriage put away and the horses settled in the barn, they'd all be in the kitchen, and Mam would be passing out pie while Martha poured coffee and Barbie bounced the little one up and down to make him laugh, joking the while with the other kids. Sarah's kids always did like Barbie because of the way she cut up with them, Peter the six-year-old especially. When he and Barbie got going, you could hardly tell one was older than the other.

Of course everyone talked a mile a minute, sometimes English but mostly Dutch because Sarah's kids knew it better, and the grown-ups seemed to slip into it naturally when they got wound up. I could understand it well enough, but Barb and Martha and I mostly talked English. It strikes me the kitchen must have sounded like the tower of Babel, with the mix of English and Dutch flying around till you wondered if you should open the door and let the noise out.

I don't remember if it was English or Dutch Sarah used to say she'd be having another baby before long, but I remember how upset Mam was. "You're not getting any younger," Mam said. "You know it gets harder the older you are."

Mam always worried over my sisters having babies. Martha said it was because she'd had such a hard time and told me once how Mam screamed and moaned when I was born and how, little as she was, she'd run out and hid in the haymow to get away from it. I guess having babies in those days was enough to scare any woman, but Sarah seemed to take it in stride. At least John did. "If God sends them, there's not much we can do," he said. Mam gave a little frown, but Sarah smiled at her and said, "I guess if you could have thirteen, I can manage a seventh one."

Mam shook her head as much as to say it was harder than Sarah made out. "And as soon as July!" she said. Still frowning, she turned to John. "I hope you get someone in this time to help out," she said. "With six already, Sarah has too much on her."

"We still got the farm to pay off," John said. "We'll see, when it's time."

Ellie spoke up then. She was Sarah's oldest and not many years younger than me, about eleven. "Mammy says I can look after things," Ellie said, and Lizzie who was nine said, "I'm going to help, too."

"You see what good help I have," Sarah said. "I guess we'll make do."

Barbie had been fussing over the three-year-old but taking it all in. She looked up from wiping the little one's mouth, dimples showing like she had everything all figured out. "I know what," Barb said. "If Mam can spare me, I'll come over and help out."

Mam was still upset over Sarah's news, I guess, and still frowning. "A lot of good that would do," Mam said, mad because John Eby hadn't promised to hire someone. "You'd be good enough at playing with Peter and fussing with the little ones, but how much do you know about running a farm and looking after a new baby? Your sister needs real help, not another child in the house."

I thought for a minute Barbie was going to cry, and the dimples went out like someone closed a shutter. "Mammy, I ain't that helpless," she said. "You always act like I'm a baby, but I think I do a good bit."

Mam sighed and tapped her fingers on the table so you couldn't tell if she was mad at herself or at Barbie. "Sarah needs real help this time," she said to Barbie before turning back to Sarah like she was looking for an ally. "You don't think Barbie would be help enough, now, do you?"

"She might," Sarah said. "If it came to that, I'd have her."

At that Barb's dimples came back, and before long she had the kids all talking and giggling while Martha redded off the table and Mam and Sarah got the beds ready, Mam calling to Barbie from the spare room not to get the children over-excited so they couldn't sleep.

In those days everyone kept a spare room for visiting, because it was a smart drive if you had family as far away as Weaverland. Young people just married used it too, spending the first month or so visiting from one house to another. Ours was in back behind the parlor, and like the parlor, it had all the things in it too good to use for ourselves, like the best bed with Mam's best quilt on it and a kind of metal rack covered with lace fastened on the headboard that pulled down to cover the pillows above the square quilt. The spare room had the cradle in it, too. At a year and a half, Sarah's youngest was almost too big for it now, but Mam said he might as well sleep in it while he could because he'd be sharing a bed with the others soon enough. The other kids got tucked in all over the house, the boys in the trundle bed where I slept before Mart went West, and the girls all tumbled together on a pile of feather beds Mam made up for them on the floor in Martha and

Barb's room. The little girls must have gone right off, but I heard Ellie and Barb whispering through half the night till Martha spoke up, sharp and bossy, saying she was tired and wanted some sleep.

The next morning was a bustle, too, with everyone getting ready for church, Martha washing faces and Barb braiding hair and Mam brushing the boys when they'd stand still long enough. "I must be getting old," she said to Sarah, "because I don't know how you manage." She didn't say so, but I think she was as happy as not to be staying home, Sarah with her, to put boards in the table and get dinner ready and catch her breath while the rest of us piled into the carriages and trotted off to church.

Hershey's Church—some still called it Hess's—sat beside the Pequea not far off the Newport Road. It looked a lot like Paradise or any other Mennonite church, plain brick with windows set in regular panes in a row on either side, the inside divided into two sets of benches with an aisle between and the preachers' platform at the far end. If Paradise was our home church, Hershey's was special, partly because it had the graveyards, the new one where my granddaddy was buried in the first row and the old one down the road where my two little sisters were. That was part of what made it special, but it was more that it sat on a slope above the creek with trees all around it and looked over the fields rolling on the other side, making a sort of picture around the farms you could see there, with the Hess place Lillie and I moved into forty years later right in the center.

But the thing we boys liked about it was the creek down below, where the bank fell into a tangle just beyond the fence. We used to think it looked like Africa down there, and we'd line up and hang over the fence till the pickets hurt our bellies, straining to see into the trees. The tramps had a place there, we knew, and we'd dare each other to throw stones down, our scalps prickling when we remembered the time Bob's Galen threw one, and a bum came out of the trees, cursing and scrambling up the bank while we watched, too scared to run till he got almost to the fence, when we all turned and hightailed it into the church faster than we ever went in before.

That Sunday we didn't have time to look for bums and got there just in time for service, after the confusion of Sarah's brood getting ready. I got stuck in the same bench with John Eby, where Pap told me to sit so I could help keep the little boys in order. From what I could tell, John liked the sermon well enough. It was on what Jacob Hershey generally preached about, dedicating our lives so we accepted the burden and lived like Christ (*der Herr*, Jacob Hershey called Him), and not fighting even in our hearts, but always using Christ as our model so we'd love our enemies enough to forgive them.

I liked what he was saying, but it was hard concentrating on all that German, with the windows open so the air came in and I could look out over the creek and see the fields and the trees moving a bit in the breeze. Every once in a while a baby would start to make some noise, its voice floating over the benches till the mother tapped her hand over its mouth and shushed it or else got up and carried it to the back where they kept a couple cradles to quiet the babies too little to hush.

A honeybee flew in through the window and buzzed up and down the glass and I wondered why it wasn't smart enough to go over the sash and out, and then I was thinking about Pap's German Bible and then about the old graveyard down the road where my sisters were buried near the middle with the other children and then about the old tombstones at the far end, where the birthdates all started with seventeen and our name was spelled Hersche in funny German letters.

I hadn't quite dreamed across the ocean to Switzerland when the preacher said "Amen," and the whole church rustled with the standing up and turning around. I was settling myself when I caught John Eby fixing me with a look. It made me remember what Martha said, that John Eby thought the Hersheys were wild and had really moved up to Weaverland to get Sarah away from us.

But I forgot that when we started to sing, the preacher giving the hymn and then the chorister standing up near the front with his fork and starting us.

We were proud of our singing at Hershey's, and looking back I know why. It's been years since I've heard anything like it, the bar or so till we'd all joined in and then the different parts rising through the church, the men's and women's strong against each other the way they were from sitting on opposite sides, so each line was strong and separated, and you could hear the women's voices at the top, thin and clear and half like they were singing through their noses, and the deep bass rumble from the men at the bottom, with the other parts clear in between. Hearing it, you knew we were all giving our separate strengths like the grapes in the communion wine to one stream that swelled through the church and floated out the windows and across the creek and over the fields all around.

I was happy they'd picked "Siloam." They've taken it out of the hymnals now, and nobody sings it, but it's still my favorite, with what it says about living and the sweet sadness of the sound and the words:

> By cool Siloam's shady rill
> How fair the lily grows
> How sweet the breath beneath the hill,
> Of Sharon's dewy rose!

Lo! such the child whose early feet
The paths of peace have trod,
Whose secret heart, with influence sweet,
Is upward drawn to God.

By cool Siloam's shady rill
The lily must decay;
The rose that blooms beneath the hill
Must shortly fade away.

And soon, too soon, the wintry hour
Of man's maturer age
Will shake the soul with sorrow's pow'r,
And stormy passion's rage.

Through all that pretty singing, I saw John Eby frowning. I thought at first it was because the hymn was English. It was only after church was over and we were all outside that I remembered. He didn't approve of any such fanciness as singing in parts.

But under the trees, with the sun sparkling and a breeze dancing across the creek and ruffling the women's skirts, it didn't matter. Barbie and Martha were over by the women's door where people were talking to them and admiring Sarah's girls, who were smiling back but tossing their braids now and then to look over their shoulders for Galen and Hon and the other cousins off with the men. My brother Hen was by himself close to the carriage shed, looking over the fence at the grave markers, and Pap was talking to old Peter Eby, making sure he counted on coming home to dinner.

It didn't take long till Sam and I found each other, Hon and Charl close to us as bedbugs for fear of missing something, and Bob's Galen, too. He was nine and always acting like he was a cousin instead of a nephew, often enough that Sam and I told him to run along and play. He'd grin back and say, "Yes sir, Uncle Silas, Cousin Sam," not budging any more than Charl and Hon did. Of course, with an audience like that, Sam and I had to make whatever we were doing sound extra important, to let the little boys know that we were almost grown-up and could do things on our own they weren't allowed to.

That Sunday, I remember, Sam and I were full of the trip we were planning to Lancaster and bragging some on how we were getting our pictures taken. Charl was mad that he wasn't going and said, "That's not much," and Hon asked if we could get him any of the city papers that weren't sent out to the county. But Galen grinned from that wide mouth of his. All that sure sounded grown-up, he said, and I knew he wasn't any more impressed than he ever was.

By then the men were walking towards the carriage shed. Pap called over for me to hurry on, and soon we were backing out Bluebell and Star, handing up the women, and trotting on home again, a line of carriages stretching before and behind in the May sun.

A good number of them followed us all the way home, too, because Sarah and John didn't come often, and when they did, Mam made sure to invite Bob and Enos and their families, besides Peter the Hermit. It wasn't right for the children not to see each other, she said, and Peter Eby needed a good meal and a chance to visit with his son. That made for enough company to fill up the kitchen, the dinner table stretched out so far you expected it to sag in the middle, and another beside the door for the children.

Mam said if the family grew much more she'd have to start using the washhouse for a summer kitchen and put the overflow out there, but with Lizzie and her batch off at the seashore and Mart away in the West, we still fitted, Sarah's youngest in a highchair and Enos's third asleep in the cradle in the spare room. Soon as I got in the door, you can bet I did a quick count to see that there weren't more than eight plates on the baby table and I'd be able to sit with the grown-ups.

Mam and Sarah had been on the lookout for us and started putting food on the table even before we got in: platters of fried beef and ham, and corn pudding and potato pies yellow with saffron and boats of gravy and relishes, like redbeet eggs and bread-and-butter pickles and chow-chow and Mammy's jams and butter for the bread we always wiped our plates with. It was a bustle till Galen and I carried in the green chairs from the front room and we all got arranged around the food. Then Pap put his head down and the talk stopped, even the little ones not making a sound, though I knew they were peeking out like I was to see when Pap would put his head up again and we'd know the prayer was over and we could start passing.

Not much got said then, food coming by so fast you hardly had time to eat what you'd already dished up. It wasn't till the plates were emptied and the platters on another round that much talk got going. We were more leisurely over seconds, and tongues were clacking all around the table by the time we got to Mammy's pies and the cake.

"I hear Bishop Eby's been visiting over at the Blue Rocks," John said, while Mammy and the girls chatted away to Sarah and fussed over the little one in the highchair, not noticing what was said at our end of the table.

"At least he didn't get skinned," Pap answered, and John Eby chuckled.

"He probably deserved to, meddling in that mission business," John said. My brother Enos looked up from cleaning his plate. I knew that he thought a good bit of the bishop and went along with most of what Ike Eby was trying to do. "I don't see that it's meddling," Enos said.

Mammy looked across from the other end of the table where she was talking with Sarah and putting a spoon into the baby's mouth. She always could tell when Enos was riled, but all she did was give him a look and turn back to the baby. "It's our Christian duty to start missions," Enos said but staring at his plate because he'd caught Mam's eye. "The Apostle Paul's authority enough."

"It's not the old way," John said. "There's never been change like the last years, and these missions are one more. When did we ever meddle like this?"

"Missions aren't meddling. They're duty," Enos said, still staring at his plate. John Eby looked at his pap. "*Was sagst du, Vater?*" he said, and old Eby looked at us with eyes so sharp under that white cap of hair that I'd have guessed he and Pap were cousins if I hadn't known already. It was funny to think of him on his farm over by the Gap and Pap down here by Strasburg and Ike Eby near Kinzers on his farm with the big white pillars that looked to hold up the barn, the three of them cousins and making a kind of triangle with Peter Eby and the bishop on opposite corners from each other and Pap somewhere in between, following where the church went but his feelings closer to Peter Eby's.

"I wish they'd keep to the old ways," Peter Eby said. I leaned over my plate to hear, quiet as he said it. Everyone at our end of the table was listening, my brothers Hen and Bob breaking off what they were saying and Mammy and Sarah looking down the table so you could tell they were trying to hear too.

"First the English and the Sunday schools, and now the missions," old Eby said, "not to mention these preachers Ike Eby keeps bringing in from the West, all talking about conversions and inner lights and such gibberish that it's like listening to people from the moon."

My brother Bob struck in then. He was a bit over thirty

and already part bald like Enos, but the skin over his skull was a lot cooler. His farm was off the Newport Road not far from the church, and already he was a school director. "Like it or not, it's easy to see what Ike Eby's about," he said. "He figures if he imitates them, he'll keep the young people from going off to other churches. You know how many go to evening services at St. John's." He didn't look at me, but I squirmed, remembering walking over nights with Biney and the girls, Biney being het on catching them and Pap not letting us take the buggy.

Peter Eby nodded. "I know what Ike Eby's about," he said, "but that doesn't make it right. Things are in a fine pass when the children lead and the fathers follow because they can't keep them in line any other way. Give Ike Eby his head, and pretty soon our church will be as proud as any. We may not have colored glass and pipe organs yet, but that's what he's taking us to."

Pap was studying his coffee where he'd poured it into the saucer by his cup stand, but Enos's chin was sticking out, and I could see he was still mad. "I don't see what that's got to do with missions," he said. Old Eby gave him a sharp look and bent his head. "When you start such changes, who but the Lord knows where it will end?" he said softly.

Everybody at the table was quiet for a minute. Then Sarah's John said, "You should move up to Weaverland with us," and from the other end of the table Mam said John's pap needed another helping. Barbie got up and carried over the cake plate. "Have another slice, Cousin Peter," she said.

It was a funny moment, and I've always remembered it, a kind of picture in my memory, Barbie so dark and blooming bent over that white-headed old man, and him leaning back in his chair so she could reach his plate. He smiled at her, like he remembered the song we'd sung at church, with Barbie the child in the second verse, and she smiled back while she dished him the last slice of cake. Then she moved off and the rest of us finished. Old Eby didn't say anything else, only pressed his fork against his plate to pick up the crumbs.

We all got up then, the men moving into the front room and beyond to the parlor that Mammy had opened because we had company, the women bustling around the table and clattering dishes at the dry sink, all talking in bunches and catching up on news and babies and ailments. I went out on the porch with Bob and Enos and Hen, while Galen and Sarah's Peter hung beside me, trying to get me away from my brothers and out to the yard to push them on the swing.

My brothers didn't seem to mind if I was there, though Bob and Enos were both twice my age. As for Hen, he was used to me hanging around. They all three stood there with their hands in their pockets, Bob and Enos looking down over the fields and talking about how the wheat was coming and whether the ground was right for putting in the corn. Both of them being on farms, it was like all they could see was the fields, Enos especially, but I could see that Hen was looking beyond to where the sky hit the ridge and that he had something else he wanted to talk about.

He waited till Bob and Enos were quiet a minute, calculating over their crops and tobacco beds. Then Hen said, "I've been thinking. What would you say to my taking the examination and getting myself a school?" Looking at Bob, he went on, "Think I'd have a chance of passing and getting one?"

"Think you got time to teach school and farm too?" Enos asked, not really making it a question. He and Bob were both stocky like the Buckwalters and about of a size, but Enos always looked thicker, like he was growing out of whatever patch he was standing on. When I think back, none of his kids left the church or the land. He seemed half mad that Hen would even talk about being a school teacher.

"Where'd you get that idea?" Bob asked. Hen knew his was a real question and answered that talking with Lizzie's Harry at the seashore had made him think about some things.

"I always knew we should have locked that girl in the root cellar before we let her run with Harry Hess," Enos said.

Bob didn't pay any attention to Enos. "I don't know," he said. "You got enough education and you're smart enough. If you got the energy, more power to you. I'd be glad to put in a word."

Hen's face relaxed, and he looked happier than I'd seen him in a month or so. I almost thought he was going to pump Bob's hand and thank him, but he just said, "I'd appreciate it." Bob had half turned and was looking out at the ridge. "I'll say something to Captain Frew and find out when Milt Brecht will be around to give the test," Bob said. Enos frowned. "One way or another, I knew Lizzie would bring trouble on the family," he said.

Someone opened the porch door, and I looked around to see John Eby. He cocked an eyebrow and said in Dutch that he thought he'd join us for some fresh air. All of a sudden the thought of more talk, in Dutch too, was more than I had a stomach for. I looked across the grass where the kids were laughing around the swing, Ellie pushing Enos's two and barely making the chain bend, while Galen shouted at her to push harder.

"Guess the kids need some help," I said and headed across the yard, trying to look at least a little dignified, while Bob chuckled behind me and ahead Ellie called me to come help, and Galen shouted, "Hurry on, Sike, if you're not too big to play with nephews and nieces!"

VII.

It was Saturday after Sarah's visit that Sam and I took off for our trip to town. I remember Pap saying I'd better kick up my heels and get spring out of my system fast, because come Monday we'd be planting corn.

Sam and I walked together to the train at Paradise, where we saw Bishop Eby and his wife and ducked out of their way so we wouldn't have any constraint while we spent our shares of tobacco money our paps gave us after the Lorillard man came by and bought our crop, little as he paid that year. Lancaster was only eight miles away, but it seemed like the end of the world, the train going fast to get there and the city so different from our life, with the rich people who ran things and all those Catholics on Cabbage Hill.

We made the most of our day, though. First we got our pictures taken, but then our luck gave out. At Hager's we ran into Bishop Eby and his wife.

Sam and I both tried to act like we were as glad to see him as he was to see us. His wife was right behind him, holding one of the little girls by each hand and all smiles. Bishop Eby already had a grown family by the time he married her, and I remember Pap grumbling that young as she was, he wondered the bishop didn't just adopt her. But it was the bishop we had to contend with, coming along and spoiling our day like that. At least that's the way we saw it, being boys, though I think now we should have been pleased that he even bothered with us.

"Elizabeth noticed you at the station, and I'd been hoping we'd run into you," the bishop said after he'd asked how everyone was. "I have some news for you. We may have a visitor next month, a man from the West coming to preach the Word of God. I wanted you to know so you could tell your families and plan on coming to hear what he has to say."

He must have caught the looks Sam and I sneaked at each other, both knowing what my pap especially would say to that, but he didn't let on, just kept talking cool as could be about how popular evening services seemed to be with young people, from the crowds they drew over at St. John's. He looked at us sort of like he was meditating while he went on to say it was time we had more of our own. "From what I've heard of him, Amos Wenger should be able to put some life back in our church," he said.

I half thought the bishop winked at us when he said that, but I wasn't sure, and his wife started talking then, telling us Wenger had taught school and gone to the Moody Institute and made quite a name for himself. "We hope he'll be able to harvest some souls here," she said, while the bishop rubbed his chin and looked at us like he was studying how much we'd bring at auction. By then Sam and I were both so fidgety that we'd have promised just about anything to get out of there, so when the bishop asked could he count on seeing us if there were special meetings next month, we said "Yes sir" quick as could be. He smiled and reached out to shake hands before he turned away and moved towards the shoe department, his wife and kids behind him. Sam and I stood by the collars for a minute, then headed for the door lickety-split.

Still, that turned out to be the most satisfying part of our day, because after that we ran into two fellows from Christiana who took us to a pool hall and gave us a ride home, though they made us dig into our pockets and pay at every toll station on the Pike.

Walking home, Sam and I didn't say much, knowing our day hadn't ended as well as it began. It was dark, too. The moon was past the quarter, but you couldn't see much of it, and the air was close as if the whole sky was leaning on our shoulders. Off to the south we saw flashes now and then. "Heat lightning," I said and Sam said, "Maybe so." Neither of us said much more until we got to Sam's place. "At least we made a day of it," he said before he turned up the lane and I headed on towards home.

I was halfway down our lane before I saw I wasn't the only Hershey getting in late. Dark as it was, there was a light on in the kitchen, and the lightning made enough flashes that I could see a buggy drawn up by the house. I heard voices but was pretty close before I could tell what they were saying or even realize for sure that it was Barbie sitting in the buggy with her young man, Enos Barge. When I saw that, I realized I should have been stamping my feet or singing or talking to myself or something, but by then I decided it would be even worse to let them know I was there, when I was close enough to hear what they were saying.

"Enos, I just don't want to," I heard Barbie say. I remembered that she and Biney had gone out to a party at Ella Leaman's and wondered to myself who Biney went with this time, but then the lightning flashed again, and I saw Enos had his hands on Barb's shoulders, trying to draw her against him, while she was pushing him away.

I was still trying to decide what to do about being there when I heard Enos say, "Barbie, I want to marry you. Don't you even like me?"

"I don't know," Barbie said, and through the dark I could tell she was still pushing him even before I heard her say, "Let me go!"

"Will you marry me or won't you?" Enos said, and the lightning flashed closer, right over the south ridge, so I could see them struggling, her eyes wide and dark and his whole face tight like there was a fist inside it. I knew Barbie was no weakling and half expected her to give him a shove that would knock him over the back of the buggy, but she didn't. While I watched he pulled her up till their faces were against each other and I could hear gasps, like Enos was crying while he held her against him.

He must have loosened his grip about then, because she walloped him one and jumped out of the buggy so fast Enos didn't seem to know what happened. I heard a smack and a scramble, and when the lightning flashed again Barb was standing at the gate, her face all squeezed up so I knew she was crying. "How dare you kiss me like that!" she said, and the funny thing was, it was like she was whispering at the top of her lungs, being ashamed even to say it out loud. "How could you!" she said again. Nothing moved in the buggy, so I could hardly tell it was there except that the horse shifted his feet.

"Barbara," Enos said, but she turned and ran for the house, bawling like a baby but stopping on the porch. "Don't come back, Enos Barge!" she called into the dark before she grabbed the kitchen latch and disappeared inside.

Enos stayed still a minute, like he was waiting to see if

she'd come out again. Then he swore at the horse and backed around faster than I'd ever seen him come in. He must have given a cut with the whip, because he and horse and buggy tore out the lane like they had yellow jackets after them.

I took my time going in, closing the gate after me that Barb had left hanging open and counting five over each step before I got to the porch. I even stamped my feet before I opened the door, but nobody was in the kitchen, just the kerosene light on the table turned down low where Mammy always left it till we all got home. I heard steps overhead and knew Barbie was up in her room with Martha.

I took off my shoes and outened the lamp, tiptoed upstairs, and crawled into bed beside Hen, who was snoring a bit till I pushed him over. I laid down on my back and thought about the day, wondering what to make of it all. I didn't even know I was asleep till I felt Hen crawling over me. "It's raining in," he said, and went over to the window where he stood a minute before he slammed it down and stumbled back to bed. "Guess we won't plant Monday," he said before he rolled over and went back to sleep while I listened to the rain pounding against the window.

VIII.

The corn got planted just before the locust blossoms came out, white in little bunches all through the green leaves. I always especially liked locust trees, and I think Pap did, too, because they were slender and pretty and tougher than any other tree I know. Pap laughed sometimes and said they were Hershey trees, but he could talk some when he had to cut one down.

I guess anyone who grew up in Lancaster County thought locust trees were special because we weren't allowed to go barefoot till they bloomed, and even if you were fifteen and finishing up your last year at school and too old to run barefoot like a little kid or an Amishman, you still knew that when those white flowers started hanging in the rows of spiny trees, it was summer.

I was busy the next couple of weeks after school helping to weed the tobacco bed, because that was before the steamers came round to sterilize the soil before we planted.

Martha was the best one for working the tobacco bed, even if Hen said the effort of getting her outside was hardly worth what she did. That wasn't quite fair, because Martha was good at the garden and liked to be out after the locust trees bloomed. She did her share, if she didn't jump around and fuss over things like Barbie. Pap said he didn't dare let Barb near the tobacco till it was near grown, or she'd hack it down with the thistles, but we all laughed, knowing she wasn't that careless, just filled with too much life to do things slow and careful.

That was the year Sam and I finished school, happy as could be to be done with it. Charl was jealous, but Hon seemed to think books were fine though Sam and I thought my brother Hen was setting a bad example. Of course I'd told them how Hen sat up by the kitchen lamp and fussed over books nights since he'd stopped seeing Annie Keene. Sam and I thought it was a dumb way to waste time, but Hon smiled and said he didn't see the waste if Hen would only be sleeping otherwise. Hon seemed to think studying to be a schoolteacher was a fine thing, but when Sam and I left the Blackhorse School that June, we both hoped we'd never have to open another book, and we let our eyes wander over the fields while we walked home, both thinking how good it would be to spend our time in them from now on.

Planting got complicated that year, with Uncle Elias and Aunt Annie going off visiting just when it was time to start putting in tobacco. "Elias must work at picking the wrong season for things," Mam said, but Pap said she shouldn't worry, because Elias always got things done one way or another, and he'd come home and get his crop in eventually. Mam clicked her tongue, so I could tell she was as happy as not that Uncle Elias had given another example of what a bad manager he was. She wasn't even mad he and Aunt Annie were off, because this way she could growl and grumble and have the pleasure of showing how well she could handle even two farms at a time. She didn't mind keeping an eye on Biney, either, saying as much time as that girl spent at our place, she couldn't see as it would be any different than usual.

Biney could have gone visiting with her folks, but she was afraid of being away and missing any parties. Her brother Dave was staying home, too, looking after the stock and keeping the farm from going completely to wrack and ruin, as Mam had it. Dave did most of the work at Uncle Elias's anyway, and he could look after himself, but Barb and Biney put their heads together, Biney saying she could sleep on the featherbed at our place and Barb saying she'd as soon stay over at the home place with Biney and Dave. At that, Mam gave a look at Barb and said, "Much good you'd be if a crisis came up in the middle of the night." Barbie said, "Oh, Mammy," but she didn't say anything more, because she knew what Mam was getting at.

It was old Grandmother Hershey, lying in the bed she'd been in ever since Grandpap died way back in 1883. In his will Grandpap set all his sons up with farms, but he arranged that all of them had to give money towards Grandmother's keep, and Uncle Elias and Aunt Annie had to see that she was looked after. It was like they inherited her with the farm for as long as she lived.

Grandmother hadn't been much of a problem for them when they moved in, I guess because then they had Aunt Sue living there and nursing her. Aunt Sue was forty then and not wacky, the way she got later. Or not right away, anyhow, when Grandmother first went to bed after she'd been to the funeral and seen my granddaddy laid in his grave at Hershey's Church. At first everyone thought she'd get over it and be up and around again, but she didn't, just laid in bed with Aunt Sue nursing her seven or eight years till Sue got so they were afraid they'd have to lock her in the attic.

I could remember the fuss that time, Aunt Sue in our kitchen and bawling and laughing some and then shaking and crying again, and Mam bustling around and patting her on the shoulder and saying it would be all right and she'd see to things. "I just can't stand any more," I remember Aunt Sue saying, and Mam smoothing a shawl over her shoulders and saying, "There now, there," in the voice she used when one of us kids was sick. "Of course you can't, and at your time of life," Mam said, after she'd shooed Martha out of the kitchen, not knowing Barbie and I were seeing what went on from behind the stair door.

Mam did see to things, too. It was right after that Aunt Sue moved over to Uncle Menno's, and they got in Mrs. Divet, everyone in the family reaching deeper into their pockets to pay the extra expense whether they liked it or not when Mam got after them and put Pap onto it. From then on Aunt Sue got along all right. At least Mam said she did and that she just acted funny because of her hearing, but I never knew.

Mammy wasn't so charitable about Grandmother Hershey. Pap said she was worn out ofter working all those years and having twelve babies. You couldn't blame her for running down after all that, he said, but Mam pursed her mouth and said having babies was bad but you didn't give up and go to bed. "And look what she did to Sue," Mam would say. She thought Grandmother was faking, especially because Doc Leaman said she could have been up and doing for herself anytime she wanted for the last thirteen years.

Whether Pap was right and she was sick or whether Mammy was and she was just lazy and too contrary to get up, Grandmother Hershey was lying in bed over at Uncle

Elias's, and we all knew she was the hard part about looking after things while he and Aunt Annie were away, mostly because of that pipe of hers. Mrs. Divet was getting pretty tottery, and we were all afraid Grandmother would burn the house down before Mrs. Divet looked over her glasses to notice. "Somebody has to be there quick with a bucket," Mammy said when we were getting plans together. She said Biney could stay home or sleep at our place, as she pleased, but Barbie wasn't sleeping in that house. Instead, Mam would sleep at Elias's and look to the fire brigade. Of course Pap said he would too and be ready to pass her the bucket.

All that made for a pretty disruptive tobacco planting, with Pap and Mam shifting between houses and Martha and Barb mostly running ours, while Hen grumbled. Come to think of it, I did, too. As for Biney, she slept in the featherbed with Barbie and Martha, talking and giggling through the night so I could hardly sleep with two doors between me and them. Hen didn't seem to notice it so much because he always fell asleep just after he came upstairs from studying over his books. But Mam and Pap were home early enough every morning, and we got on with the planting.

It took the bunch of us to get it done fast and right, Pap moving ahead down a furrow with a kind of a compass he walked down the row and shifted from one leg to another to mark where the plants went, and Hen and Barbie and me trailing behind him one after the other, me with the dibble to make the holes, Barbie dropping plants, and Hen pouring water and stamping them into place. Ben Gray, Pap's lead mule, walked alongside with the spring wagon, keeping pace without being told and stopping whenever Barb went for a new bunch of plants or Hen needed to fetch water from the milk can, mules being smart that way, even if Ben got confused now and again whether to keep up with

Pap or with Barb and Hen and me, when Barb would stop and stare up at the clouds or off at the trees by the fencerow like she'd forgot where she was.

I never minded pauses, and Barb was pretty to look back at in her red sprigged work dress and a yellow sunbonnet with a ruffle on the back to keep her neck from getting sunburned. She'd taken off her shoes because she said she liked the feel of dirt under her feet. Pap said he guessed it was all right since there were only her brothers to see her. I could tell he was going to say more, till he saw her face and knew she didn't want any more jokes about Enos Barge, so instead he commented that she should be tough enough by now not to mind the stones.

You could tell, when she stopped, it wasn't because of them. A couple times Hen called her to hurry on, and she'd drop plants like a windmill to the end of a row. Then she'd stop and stare off again, a little frown over her nose like she was working out a riddle from the Saturday newspaper. "I wonder what Lizzie's doing now," she said to me once when she stopped. "It must be cool and nice by the seashore," and she licked a little mustache of sweat off her lip.

"I guess Lizzie's tending the kids," I said, "and doing the washing and putting up preserves in a hot kitchen."

"Oh, Silas," Barbie said, and pouted while she bent back to the row, dropped a few plants, then stood and stared off again.

Hen always did have a short fuse. Finally, when he almost bumped into her, he said, "Barbara Hershey, do you have molasses between your toes?" I remember that he said it sharp, but I remember more how Barb looked when she turned around to him, that funny fringe of dark hair stuck against her skin and her face rosy but sort of loose, like it had surprised her by wanting to cry and she hadn't had time yet to tell it not to. Her lips shook for a minute while they decided what they were going to do before she tightened them and squeezed her eyes shut to bring the frown back over her nose. "Don't scold, Hen," she said, "when I have the headache so."

I could see Hen was wishing he hadn't spoken, and the three of us stood beside Ben Gray while he flicked his tail and stamped to move the flies off his flanks. Pap was a quarter row ahead by then, but when Hen called he turned back and asked what was wrong. "Barb has the headache," Hen said. Hen was like that, making up without apologizing, but Barb knew he was sorry and looked half ashamed she'd made him feel bad. Her mouth shook again, and she said she was sorry for not keeping up. "I guess we can do without you," Pap said. "You go in and lie on the settee till you feel better." She looked at Pap and at Hen, then handed me her plants and turned back across the field, her red dress making a picture against the ploughed earth. I watched her for a minute and saw her draw a dirty fist across her face, then draggle on towards the house.

"She's touchy enough lately," Hen said, but Pap gave him a look, leaning on the compass frame with the other hand tucked under his arm while he made a noise in his throat. "Must run in the family," Pap said, and turned back to pacing out the row.

We had the better part of the tobacco in by Grandmother Hershey's birthday. "I guess David can use a good supper for a change," Mammy said. She carried over some ham and made sure Biney got ready a good mess of sugar peas and new potatoes from Aunt Annie's garden. "Mrs. Divet can carry that to your mother instead of stewed crackers," Mam said. "I don't think it will hurt her digestion any." Mammy took a cake, too, and that was special because we ate pies most of the time. "Your mother is sure to like that, anyway," I heard her say.

We had a good supper in Aunt Annie's kitchen. Mam

said it was as well she'd brought an extra mess of peas from her garden to go along with Aunt Annie's, or Dave would have emptied the bowl the first time round. "Sure beats stewed crackers," Dave said, and we all laughed, because Mrs. Divet had gone out to take the tray in for Grandmother, and it was a joke what a bad cook she was.

"Mrs. Divet seems to be failing since the winter," Mammy said, frowning. "She hardly lifts her feet now, just shuffles along from one room to the other. David, do you notice much difference?"

Dave looked up from his third helping of sugar peas, a fork in one hand and a piece of bread in the other to sop up the milk Mam always served them in. "Nah," he said. "She looks the same to me as ever, only now she burns the butter before she pours it over the crackers."

Barbie and I started to chuckle and Pap grinned, but Mam looked worried, and Biney sat up from saying something in Martha's good ear. Her mouth was wide like Sam's so the more she tried to make it serious, the more it looked like she was making a joke. "I noticed, Aunt Barbara," Biney said, while I snickered just because it was hard to take Biney seriously in those days. "And you needn't snicker at me, Sike," Biney said, trying to hold her mouth like a schoolmarm's but making it all the more like it was clamped over a joke.

"Straighten up, Silas," Pap said, so I looked down at my plate while Biney told how Mrs. Divet had started putting the dirty dishes from Grandmother's tray into the blanket chest, till her mam said it was like hunting for a broody hen's nest every time they wanted to wash the dishes. Then she looked at me and bobbed her head as much as to say she could be as grown-up as anyone.

Mammy sighed. "Old as she's getting, I'm afraid we won't be able to count on her much longer," she said to Pap. We were all quiet till she cut the cake.

As soon as we finished, Hen left to get back to his books. While the girls were washing up, the rest of us sat on at the table till Mrs. Divet came shuffling out from the other side of the house and Pap said he'd better look in on Grandmother. Sometimes I think he was the only one in our family who really liked her, but Pap had never stopped being close to his mam. Often in the evenings he'd disappear for an hour or so, and we'd know he'd gone over to see her and was sitting on the painted chair beside her bed, talking with her in German and getting her advice on anything that was bothering him. Mam shook her head now and then and wondered what they could have to talk about, but Pap smiled and said the old girl still had her wits about her.

Pap had been with her nearly half an hour, and the girls had finished redding up when Mam said Barb and Martha and I had better wish Grandmother a happy birthday. She had half the house, but her bed was made up downstairs in what should have been the parlor, so everything there seemed turned around, like Sarah and John's church where the preacher stood at the singing table in the middle instead of at a pulpit at the end. I didn't like the way it smelled, either, that funny smell old people have that I used to notice and wrinkle my nose against. I always felt like taking five or six extra lungfuls of air before I went in, and that time I must have stood in front of the door a full half minute before Martha said, "Go on, Silas, and get it over with."

"Oh, you two," Barbie said, knocked, and was into Grandmother's room, Moss and me straggling through the door behind her. Pap looked up from beside the bed. *"Hier sind die Kinder, Mutter,"* he said.

Grandmother was lying in the middle of the room on a kind of hospital bed. Mrs. Divet had propped pillows up behind her, and Pap must have helped her crank up the bed so Grandmother would be sitting up, or as near as she ever came to it. I remember the shutters were half closed and it was dusky in there except for a long yellow ray that fell across the foot of the bed and made it harder to see in the shadows everywhere else.

At first all I could see when I looked at her was a big white mound from the white pillows and white sheets and Grandmother white against them. She hadn't been outside to speak of for thirteen years, and her face was white, and her hair too. Mrs. Divet combed it for her and put it into a bun, but Grandmother didn't wear a cap. I guess she didn't see the need, when she never wore anything but a night-gown, and that was white, too, except for darker spots where the dye hadn't been quite bleached out of the bags it was made from, and charred places up the front like little brown footprints leading from where there were more of them over the top of the sheet, burns where she'd dropped the ashes out of her pipe.

She was a big woman and seemed to take up the length of the bed, but she wasn't fat, only big and seeming even bigger from all that white so you lost track of what was her and what was pillows and what was bed all in a white pile together.

She barely moved her head to look at us, as though turning it the whole way took too much strength, but her eyes moved all right, pale blue and clouded, the way old people's eyes get, but sharp, like the strength she saved not moving was stored up somewhere behind them. While we all said hello and wished her happy birthday, she rolled her eyes towards Pap. "*Können die Kinder nicht mehr Deutsch sprechen?*" she said, and Pap tucked his hands under his arms and said, "*Nur ein Bissel, Mutter. Nur ein Bissel.*"

She lay and stared at us then, not saying anything one way or another, just looking us over out of those whitish-blue eyes of hers while I fidgeted and shuffled my feet, wondering if she really was sick or if she'd been lying there all those years out of laziness and contrariness, the way Mam and Moss said. It made me feel funny to see her and remember how old she was, that she was born as long ago as the people under the stones near the back of the old graveyard, and to remember who her daddy had been, because her pap, Peter Eby, had been the biggest bishop in all Pennsylvania. The Great Mennonite Bishop of Pequea, they called him, and people still talked about him. When Grandmother was little he was bishop for Canada, too, and rode up there a couple times to look after the churches. The way people talked, Peter Eby had built the Mennonite church with his own hands. It was strange to me to think Pap was named for him.

But it was stranger to think that Grandmother was his daughter and that she'd spent sixty years married to a Mennonite preacher, when all I ever remember was her lying there white like a ghost—except that no ghost was ever so big or smoked a pipe. She was taking little puffs from it while she looked at us, and I guess all three of us were looking at the pipe, like always.

Grandmother wasn't the only old woman who liked to smoke. My Aunt Em puffed cigars and blew smoke in Pap's face once when he visited, but watching Grandmother and her pipe was different, because she smoked it upside down, as if the corncob bowl was too heavy to hold up straight in her mouth. We all stared, watching to see when the ashes would fall out and not daring to talk or even breathe till they did. Then a little clump of fire fell onto the bedclothes, and Grandmother lifted her arm, slow, like it was too much work to raise it very fast, reached her hand towards the embers, and made little scratches against them with her fingers. Right beside me Barbie sighed. Grandmother kept her eyes on us and didn't look to see if she'd left a scorch on the sheet, just rolled her head half towards Pap.

"They've grown some, don't you think?" Pap asked her. Grandmother didn't answer right away, as though she had to gather the words together before they'd come out. When they did, it always gave me a jolt, because her words were clear and sharp, even if what she said sounded queer enough.

Slowly, Grandmother reached up and took the pipe out of her mouth. "The boy favors you," she said then, "and the older girl some, too. But the other one,"—and I knew she meant Barbie—"that one looks like me."

Grandmother said that every time we saw her, and Barbie and I always laughed over it afterwards, because neither of us could imagine Grandmother ever looking like Barbie. I looked sideways at Barb, all dark and pretty and the color in her face from working outside, and I could hardly keep from laughing. I know now I was at an age for foolishness, but all I could do then was bite my lip and hope I wouldn't explode till I got out of that room, while I felt my neck getting red from the holding in. Martha must have noticed, because she gave me a smart jab with her elbow, but Grandmother didn't seem to. At least she kept her eyes on Barbie while she said to Pap, "You don't remember that, almost seventy-five years back, before you were born or the others either. Your girl favors me when I was sixteen and got married to your pap. I had a baby when I was seventeen."

Grandmother hadn't moved her head or her eyes, but all of a sudden I knew she wasn't talking to Pap any more, but to Barbie, her eyes sharp and keen like she was seeing more than the rest of us could. I was glad they weren't looking at me, even if now I didn't feel much like laughing. "I had eleven more babies after that," Grandmother said, "and that changes you some." Her eyes seemed to fade then, and it was like she was talking to the bed or the room or the house instead of to us. "But then lots else has changed since then," she said.

She held out her pipe to Pap. "Are they too grown up now for the candy?" Pap smiled while he took the pipe and handed her a covered dish from the stand beside the bed. She took off the lid and laid it beside her on the burned sheet, then reached in the bottom and counted out candy, rounds of peppermint and spearmint, six for each of us. I could almost feel Martha making a face while she held out her hand for Grandmother to put some in it, but we all said thank you, even if I knew Martha would give me hers as soon as we got outside.

We were just heading for the door when Mam opened it and stuck her head in. "Here's somebody come to visit," Mam said, holding a couple plates of cake. I saw old Peter Eby behind her. When we left, he was filling her pipe for her, and I could hear a steady stream of low talk in German while we crossed the hall back to the kitchen. I wondered what they were saying to each other, but they were both old, after all, and both of them were Ebys.

Just as we got to the kitchen Barbie touched my arm. "Do you think she really has been sick all this time?" she asked in my ear.

IX.

Summer work went on. Uncle Elias and Aunt Annie came home from their visiting, and we settled back to our regular chores, mostly cultivating just then, before the tobacco started needing more work come July. The hay wouldn't be ready to cut for another week, so Pap sent me to the house to help Mam and the girls, all of them busy enough with canning. It seems to me I told Mam I was too old to do women's work, but she said I wasn't too old to eat, was I, and headed me out to the orchard to help Barb and Martha.

When I got there, the girls were picking cherries, Martha standing near the bottom of the stepladder picking the low branches, and Barbie up in the tree, one foot braced in a fork and the other balanced on a limb so she could reach the cherries near the top. They were talking about Hen's school examination because right after dinner he'd headed down the Blackhorse Road towards Paradise. We all calculated that he was likely to be in the thick of it by now, though we wouldn't know what happened till supper time. There were four taking it besides him, and Hen said with that many there might not be enough schools to go round if he did pass. Mam sniffed even at the idea of Hen not getting either Belmont or at least Ronks, where the teachers had both left that spring. She said with his own brother on the school board and a cousin too, Dan Denlinger, he was sure to get a good one. I remember Pap said she should know better than to count on Dan Denlinger, even if his mother was a Hershey, because Dan Denlinger thought about as much of the Hersheys as Martha thought of the Ebys.

"Do you think Hen will pass?" I asked Barb. Martha had climbed up a few more rungs so her head poked through the lowest branches. "What's that you say, Silas?" she called, cocking her head so her good ear was towards us.

"Can't you miss anything, Moss?" I said, but she'd heard what I said all right and shot back that Hen was likely to manage whatever he set himself to, now that he was free of Annie Keene. "And you're better off without Enos Barge, too, Barbie," she added. Small and tidy as Martha was, even at best she was pretty stiff, and when she got in a know-it-all mood she reminded me of a stove poker. Barb had stopped picking when Martha said that about Enos and turned her face away so I couldn't see her. "Bossy Mossy," I muttered under my breath so Martha couldn't hear me. I'd have said it again, too, but Barb shied a cherry at me and stung me a good one on the neck. "Hush up, Silas," she said, and I did.

When we'd filled two milk buckets and all the kettles, we headed back to the house. Picking was one thing, but the idea of sitting down and digging out pits with a hairpin got my hackles up, and I grumbled pretty bad till Mam said I should run over to Esbenshade's and see what mail we had.

The rural delivery law had passed that spring, but it hadn't gotten to us yet, and we still had to hoof it to Paradise where they had the post office in the back part of the store whenever we wanted to find out what letters we'd got.

I didn't hurry, not being overly anxious to get back to hairpins and black cherries, but kicked my toes against the dust in the road and took my time. When I came to the Paradise Hall I wondered how Hen was making out inside. Hard as I looked, I couldn't see anything but some carriages hitched outside and a fancy steam automobile so I knew Mr. Brecht was there.

We'd got two letters, one for Barb and one for Hen. Barbie's was from Mart, I could see from the Dakota postmark, but I couldn't make out the other one. It had been stamped down at the Gap, and the address was written in a hand I didn't recognize. It was something about a school, I figured, and whistled my way back to the house.

By the time I got there Barb and Martha were sitting under the grape arbor with buckets and kettles all around them. Mammy must have been setting up the canning tub inside. "Anything for me, Sike?" Barbie called. When I asked why anyone would write to her, she jumped up and tried to see what I was hiding, while I turned backwards and she ran around me, grabbing at my hand. Martha wrinkled her mouth like a prune and said we were acting like kids, but Barb gave a shout when she wrenched those letters from me. "I got one from Mart!" she said, her face going into dimples. She stood still to study over the other one. "Look at this, Martha," she said.

"It's just some letter to Hen about a school," I said, but Martha had set down her kettle and wiped her hands on her apron, frowning while she looked at the envelope Barb handed her. "What do you think, Martha?" Barbie asked.

Martha examined the postmark and the address and then held the letter up against the light. "It's sure not about a school," she said, and dropped it onto her lap like it was poison ivy. At that Barbie and I both dove for it, but Barbie was faster. We both studied it while she held it towards the sun the way Martha had. "Looks like a good long letter," she said after a minute, but that's all we could tell. "Who do you think it's from, Moss?" I asked, because I could tell she'd made up her mind.

Martha gave me a bossy sister look, much as to say she didn't talk about important things in front of a kid, but Barb said, "Go on, Martha. Sike won't tell." Martha gave me another look, this one saying I should appreciate the favor she was doing me, and Barb handed her the letter.

"See how bold that hand is?" Martha said, holding it by the tiniest corner she could manage. Barb and I stared at the address. The writing was big and covered half the envelope, but it was sort of fancy, too, with extra curlicues on the P's and the H's. Barbie's eyes got round, and she said, "You don't think it's from Annie Keene?"

"Of course it is," Martha said. "Couldn't be from anyone else." I started to ask why Annie would write when she only lived five miles away, but Martha cut me off. "I thought she let him go too easy, as if she wasn't smart enough to know a good catch when she found one. I guess she's had time to look around now and decided she can't do better, so she wants him back. That's who this letter's from, and as soon as Hen gets it, he'll put on his fancy suit and go running right back to her."

Barbie took the letter from Martha and looked at it again, little frown marks wrinkling the top of her nose. "Would it be all that bad?" she said, half like she was asking herself a question.

Martha had her head turned to catch what Barbie said, and she snapped right back, "Of course it would. As if Annie Keene was good enough for Hen!" Barbie sighed.

"You don't have to give it to him," I said, smart and sassy like I was nine or ten instead of fifteen. Martha picked up a handful of cherries and started digging out the pits, dropping them into the kettle she'd put back on her lap where they plunked on the bottom. She finished the handful and looked up. "If we're ever going to get through these cherries we'd better get on with it," she said.

"I got to see what Mart has to say," Barbie said, starting to rip open the other envelope. "Maybe you should put Hen's letter away first," Martha said half under her breath. She gave Barbie a look and added, "You might put it in the sideboard drawer, under the tablecloths." Barbie stood for a minute fiddling with the letter, then ran into the house. After she'd been inside a bit, I heard her shout into the washhouse, "Mam, Mam! We got a letter from Mart!" At that I said we'd better go in if we wanted to hear Mart's letter and lit out for the house.

Pap rescued me from the cherries to help water tobacco, and when we got in again, the women had finished the cherries and had supper set. Hen was already at the table, his head bent over his plate, but not like he was praying. Pap and I could see him while we washed up at the outside pump, but when I wondered aloud how he'd made out at the school test, Pap told me to mind my mouth. "He'll tell us in good time," Pap said. "A lot that's told has to come gentle, so don't you rush things."

Mam and the girls sat down as soon as Pap did so we could all put our heads down, but as soon as that was done Mam and Barbie jumped up again to put more things on the table and especially to help them onto Hen's plate. He let them for a while, and shoveled in food till his plate was clear the second time. In spite of what he'd said to me, I guess Pap couldn't stand it any longer by then, because he looked at Hen and said, "Well, did you pass?"

Hen poured his coffee into the saucer and took a sip. "Yep," he said. Mammy looked up from the place opposite Pap, her face warm with smiles. "Of course he did," she said, though I could tell she was relieved to hear it. "I knew you'd pass, Henry," she said. Mam always knew we'd do as well as anyone, but it was funny to see how nervous she was until we did it. "You never had a thing to worry about," she said, but Hen kept his head down. "Which school did you get?" Mam asked him.

Hen took another sip of coffee, and Pap fixed his eyes on me as much as to say he'd see me behind the tobacco shed if I opened my mouth. So I didn't. Barb and Moss didn't either, but we all stared at Hen, who finished his coffee and set down his saucer before he said to Mammy, "They didn't give me a school."

If she hadn't been so fat, I think Mam might have gone through the ceiling. "You passed the test and you didn't get a school?" she said, her eyes looking like Barbie's and her mouth round like a doughnut, as surprised as she was to hear her son hadn't got everything she expected for him. "They didn't give you a school!" she said again, like she hadn't heard right. "And you passed the test?"

"I passed, all right," Hen said, throwing his head back and talking towards the board where we hung our coats and overalls. "Brecht tested my spelling and sampled my writing and quizzed me on geography, and then he asked me about the reproductive system." Martha gasped, but Barb and I leaned over our plates. "He liked my answers well enough, and he passed me," Hen said. Barb and I sat back again.

"If you did all that, you should have got a school," Martha said, and Barbie chimed in, "Why didn't you get a school, Hen?"

Hen looked down from the coat hooks and across to Barbie. "I should have," he said. "Lord knows I should have."

"That Dan Denlinger," Martha spoke up. "I'll bet he did it."

"Never you mind, Martha," Pap said. "Whatever happened, it's God's will." He shoved back his chair and said to Mam, "I think I'll run over to see Mother." Mam nodded and got up to clear the table, and Pap tucked his hand under his elbow and went out the door. I knew he tucked the other one in too as soon as he got outside.

"Landis got the Belmont School," Hen said, and Martha said, "How could they give a school to that lummox?" "Now, Martha," Mammy said, but Hen sat staring at his empty plate, and at the empty spot on the table after Martha took it away. Barbie hadn't gotten up to help clear but stayed at the table with Hen, looking like she wanted to cry for him.

"Hen," she said real soft. "You got a letter today." She jumped up and opened the drawer to the sideboard. "I think it's from Annie Keene," she said when she handed it to him.

Hen read the letter and hitched up the buggy. Barb went to bed early with the headache, and Mam and Martha sat up working over the quilting frame, on the top Barb had pieced with the calico she'd bought from the Peddlar Lady. For myself, I went out and sat on the porch swing. I sat there till it got dark, looking at the fields rolling away before they ended at the south ridge and wondering to myself what it would be like going with a girl like Annie Keene.

X.

It stayed dry through haymaking, and Barbie spent her birthday on June twenty-third out raking hay with Mam and Hen and Pap and me. Martha stayed around the house to cook and fuss around the garden because Mammy said field work took too much strength for someone as frail as she was, but Hen muttered that Martha was about as fragile as a copperhead. There wasn't any love lost between Martha and Hen now that he was back seeing Annie Keene. Martha told him right out what she thought of Annie and of him seeing her. Mad as he looked, I thought Hen was going to hit her, but instead he squinted his eyes the way he did when he was really hopping and said in a steady voice that Martha had best never say a word like that to him again. After that she knew better than to try it, but when Hen wasn't around she grumbled how Barbie should never have given him that letter.

As for Barb, she looked confused when Martha lit into

her about Hen's letter. Sometimes she stuttered like a little kid someone caught with a spoon in the jam jar and said, after all, it was Hen's letter. Other times she hardly answered, only frowned like the whole problem was a big knot being pulled tight inside her head. Those were the times her hands would get slower and slower over the butter churn or the hay rake or whatever she was working at till she'd have to go and lie down from the headache.

She cheered up, though, when Hen asked was she interested in going in with him to have a party, and Mam said she didn't see any reason they shouldn't. Barb enjoyed fussing over that, working out couples and deciding what to say on the invitation, but Martha just pursed her lips, knowing Hen would bring Annie Keene.

Getting ready for that party kept us all scrambling, especially because all kinds of other things were going on at the same time. Hen was busy looking for schools and checking out openings he'd heard of in Bart Township, and my sister Sarah's baby was due. Mam fussed and fretted that no one was there with her. I know she didn't know whether to be more upset or relieved the Wednesday Sarah's John whipped up the drive to say Sarah had had a boy the day before. John was on his way to fetch one of his sisters, who was going to stay till Saturday a week, but Mam said Sarah would need help longer than that.

"That'll be after the party. I'll go over, Mam!" Barbie said, bouncing her foot on the buggy step. "I could go over next week and see to things for Sarah." Mammy gave a little sniff and said she'd be as likely to put the baby in the oven and tuck the bread into the cradle. Barbie stopped bouncing and pouted. I could see her feelings were hurt, though if she'd thought about it she'd have known Mam was just worried that Sarah would have someone she could count on.

"Let me know if she can't stay longer," Mammy said. "I may be able to get away for a few days." She clicked her tongue while she watched him out the lane. "I just hope John's sister can manage," she said, before we all went back to our chores.

Mammy told Pap about Sarah's baby over supper, fussing and clucking and complaining the while that John had as much Eby contrariness as old Peter the Hermit, or else he'd see that Sarah had proper help when she needed it. "I don't know how much good John's sister will be, either," Mam said. I looked at Barb, and Barb looked at me, and we both grinned, because we knew Mammy didn't think anyone could do a proper job of looking after Sarah or anyone else unless she was there doing it herself. Pap winked at me, and we all waited for Mam to finish her say with what we knew was coming next.

"I don't see anything for it except to go over to Sarah's and look after things myself," Mam said. Sober as a judge, Pap looked at Mammy and said, "If you say so, Barbara."

Of course with the party coming up Mam couldn't leave and go up to Weaverland right away. Besides, Pap managed to convince her that John's sister had always been a smart enough manager that Sarah might just be able to scrape by with her till Saturday a week, when he promised he'd drive Mam up and stay the night. So on top of threshing and Barbie and Hen's party, Sarah's new baby made more fuss for us, but even that was nothing beside the excitement about the visiting preacher Bishop Eby had told us about. Amos Wenger showed up about the same time everything else was going on. He was the one that started the changes.

We were all confused about where he came from. When he got to Lancaster the weekend before Barb's party, he'd just taken the train down from Canada, but he'd been living in Iowa, going to college, though he said he was from Virginia and had gone to normal school in Missouri and had been a preacher in Missouri and Iowa. He'd been in Chicago, too, like the bishop's wife told us, at the Moody Bible Institute. Pap said that must have been what got him so fired up, because he wasn't like any Mennonites we knew except other ones who came in from the West, like S. F. Coffman and Sam Yoder from Elkhart, Indiana. Yoder had been through Lancaster the winter before and had preached and prayed and told us how sinful we were, but he hadn't made much of an impression, because we all knew that if Mennonites from out there belonged to the same church, it was a different one than we were used to.

They'd been showing up now and then for years, some of them telling us we'd be damned if we didn't convert right away, and others saying we should staff missions and preach to the heathen and send out missionaries and go to school to learn to do more good.

When I was thirteen, one of them, Sam Coffman, had dinner at Uncle Elias's and afterwards prayed over my grandmother. I always tried to think what that must have been like. All I could imagine was Grandmother propped up in bed while she listened, puffing on her pipe and scratching at the ashes when they fell out on the bed-clothes. Afterwards when I asked Pap what Grandmother thought of Coffman, he smiled and said he guessed his mam knew better than to buy new wares from a strange peddlar.

But other people fussed, and the bishops didn't invite Coffman back to Lancaster after he gave a string of services out in Cumberland County without getting permission, there being a rule against protracted meetings. They couldn't really stop him and the others from showing up, though, invitations or not, to visit around and preach in private homes and pray over people like Grandmother Hershey, and they knew better than to try. They couldn't do anything about Coffman's new school, either, the Elkhart Institute, but when word came that it had started in the winter, there was more fuss about the fancy dress at the opening and that a Mennonite school had teachers that didn't belong to the church.

So the western preachers like Wenger weren't entirely welcome around Lancaster, in spite of Bishop Eby.

We'd all heard when he arrived to convert us local heathen and Bishop Eby let us know he'd be preaching at the Paradise Church Wednesday night of the day we heard about Sarah's baby. Of course Biney arranged for us all to go, Martha too, even if Pap wouldn't let us take the carriage, saying we could get there on our own power if we wanted to waste our time on more of Ike Eby's foolishness.

The day had been a scorcher, so hot and heavy it felt like the bottom of a well, and it hadn't cooled off much when Biney popped in. The girls were still washing up, and she fussed that they weren't dressed and we'd be late, never minding that she was usually the one to keep us waiting. She grabbed a dish towel and whisked through the drying, flinging dishes into the cupboards and then bustling the girls upstairs to help them dress, while I fixed my tie in the kitchen glass. "You look handsome enough, Sike," she called back from the steps, but as soon as she was out of sight I went back to the mirror. I was still fussing over my hair when Sam showed up, having talked Aunt Mary into keeping Charl and Hon at home for a change, and he took a turn at the mirror too. After all, in those days we went to meetings for entertainment, not to get our souls saved.

But when the five of us had walked the mile to Paradise and got ourselves settled in our benches, we weren't so sure. The visiting preacher wasn't too old, not even thirty

I'd say, but he sure was taking himself seriously and never cracked a smile when Bishop Eby introduced him. He was dressed funny, too, in a coat without lapels and with a notch out at the front. He didn't have a necktie on underneath, either, though it wouldn't have shown much under that high collar.

"Dearly beloved," he said, when he was finally standing up by himself, all of us looking at him like he came from China and studying the way he had his hair slicked and that funny coat he was wearing. I looked at Sam from the corner of my eye and Sam looked back at me the same way, then drew the corners of his mouth out wide and sober and rolled his eyes. The strange preacher cleared his throat. All of a sudden I knew he was staring right at Sam and me, eyes sharp and keen as a sparrow hawk. I jabbed Sam with my elbow, and the strange preacher said again, "Dearly beloved."

Then he launched in. He told us how he'd felt the call to preach to the heathen and how every Christian had the duty to spread the Gospel. That's what the Bible told us, and he knew we'd felt the call, too, and were interested in starting missions and in spreading the good news. Some people nodded at that, especially the Mellingers. Bishop Eby didn't, sitting up on the bench behind the lectern, but he didn't have to, because we all knew he'd asked Wenger to preach, and he didn't have to sign one way or the other to let us know he was on the side of missions and western preachers and most other new things. He kept his eyes on his knees and waited for the strange preacher to have his say, but he didn't show on his face what he thought of what Wenger said next.

Because then Wenger dropped all of that about missions and told us we couldn't expect to convert the heathen or anyone else unless we converted ourselves first. The Mellingers leaned forward at that, and Wenger went on to say he'd felt a special call to visit us because he'd heard about the evil in our church, wildness among the young people, and drinking and smoking and swearing at all ages. In fact, he said, in spite of our wanting to help the heathen, he saw from looking around that most of us weren't converted. At that he looked right at Sam and me, and I squirmed. Then he ran his eyes through the church and stared at all the young people, one after another, and asked what we'd do if the world ended tomorrow. "What would you do if Jesus came," he asked, "and He found you sitting here full of sin and worldliness and not ready for Him?"

While he was saying all that, it was hot as blazes in the church. I peeked over at Sam and could see he'd relaxed his mouth again so that he looked like he was half grinning while he waited to hear what wild things Wenger might say next. I knew we'd have lots to laugh about on the walk home, so I wiped my face with my handkerchief and sat back to listen while the preacher ranted on about how no one could face Jesus if he hadn't accepted Him and how the stars could fall any time and the world end in a shower of fire to destroy all of us, and even if we'd spent some money to convert the heathen, it wouldn't help us. We'd be separated out like chaff at the winnowing and burn forever unless we'd stood up and said to the world that we belonged to Jesus.

Looking around, I saw lots of people fanning themselves and others staring up at Wenger with their faces slack. Across the aisle I could see Martha, pale as milk and looking up to the pulpit like she'd stopped breathing. "Take a look at Moss," I whispered to Sam, and he leaned forward to get a view. "She looks ready for heaven or heat prostration," Sam whispered back while we both pretended to look sober as heathen converts.

Meantime the strange preacher hadn't stopped. "You have to let Jesus into your hearts," he said. "He's standing there, knocking at the door. Will you let him in?" Then all of a sudden he wasn't talking to us any more. "Bring Thy lost sheep into Thy fold," he said. "While we sing the song Brother Coffman wrote, we pray for the Holy Spirit to fall on the lost sheep sitting here waiting to feel Thy direction." He said that anyone who felt the call should walk up front while we sang, and he started to read a hymn. After he'd read it through once, he recited it again, verse by verse, and asked us to sing it after him. We did the best we could, but the sound was pretty thin from so few of us knowing it, and straggled through the church like it was muffled by all that heat. I know it now from hearing it so much later on:

> O weary wanderer, come home,
>   Thy Saviour bids thee come,
> Thou long in sin didst love to roam,
>   Yet still He calls thee, come.
>
>   Help me, dear Saviour, Thee to own,
>   And ever faithful be;
>   And when Thou sittest on Thy throne,
>   O Lord, remember me.
>
> Think of thy Father's house today,
>   So blest with plenteous store;
> Think of thy sinful, wandering way,
>   Then come and roam no more.
>
> Poor prodigal, come home and rest,
>   Come and be reconciled;
> Here lean upon thy Father's breast,
>   He loves His wandering child.

I never saw a church full of people so caught by surprise, but what surprised me most was hearing gasps and sobs over the singing and seeing some people get up and stumble to the front of the church. Wenger had stepped down from the preachers' platform when we started to sing and walked over to pump their arms up and down and seat them in the front bench. By the time the hymn ended he was back behind the pulpit, praying and thanking God for the first fruits of the harvest, as he called it.

Bishop Eby got up then. I couldn't help but think he looked sort of funny, as though he'd been as caught by surprise as the rest of us. I wasn't sure but that his face wasn't redder than usual, but surprised or not, as long as he'd invited Wenger, he had to thank him. While he did I couldn't help notice how he looked at the front bench where the converts were sitting, Mabel Burkhardt still sniffling so the rest of us could hear her. The bishop said we'd surely been blessed this evening and thanked Brother Wenger for his message and for God's sign that it had been answered, but he hoped we'd remember the heathen, too, and not stint on our mission work.

"That was better than a medicine show any day," Sam said when we were out under the trees. Some fellows near us laughed and asked what we thought of Mabel Burkhardt and those others finding Christ, and someone else said back that she always was a ninny. We'd picked the western preacher and his converts pretty well to pieces by the time we got Martha and Barb and Biney ready to start home again, Biney craning her neck all around, saying she'd been sure Amos Landis had planned on being there, so it took a while before we finally got her headed down the road.

By then the sky was heavy as the air. The moon wasn't up yet, and there weren't any stars to speak of. I still remember the funny feeling in my feet from putting them down and not being able to tell when they'd touch the road. I guess that's why Sam and I started to clown as soon as we got out of the light, stamping our feet down hard so we could convince ourselves we were still back where we'd always been, because on a night like that you weren't quite sure. We started to talk loud, too, and make jokes about Mabel Burkhardt. I remember that Biney laughed with us and giggled about what a goose she'd always been, and then I remember Martha snapping out at us not to make fun of what we couldn't understand.

"You're acting like a pack of ignorant children," she said. Sam said under his breath that Martha must have got some religion too, and I said, all bold in the dark, "Why didn't you go up front and accept Christ, Moss?"

"If I didn't, at least I have the sense to respect those who did," she shot back, and Sam and I hooted in the dark about all the wickedness Martha must have on her soul to be taken in by a medicine-show preacher. Biney was giggling too, and we were ready to make the rest of Martha's walk as miserable as we could until Barbie spoke up, quiet and serious. "Come on now," she said. "Lots of people paid attention to what Amos Wenger told us, and who's to say they didn't have the right of it? Even if I never had the feeling I was evil enough to need special saving, I still think it's wrong to make fun of people who do. Martha is right, and you fellows should hush up about what you don't understand."

Martha said Barb was right, Biney giggled, and Sam said that preacher might make a good living if he got paid by the piece like a cigar maker, but we didn't say much more to make fun of him or his converts while we picked our way through the dark the rest of the way home.

XI.

We didn't hear Amos Wenger the next time he preached at Paradise because that was Saturday night, and all of us had been scrambling all day to help Hen and Barbie get ready for their crush, which none of us had any doubt was a lot more important than another doomsday sermon. Mam had been turning the house inside out for a week, making me haul rugs out to the clothes line and then watching to see that I smacked them hard enough with the wire beater that she wouldn't be shamed in front of the company. She made the girls scrub down the porch, posts and all, and she was so *schusslich* over her baking that after I cleaned the coals out of the bake oven, I went and hid in the barn.

Pap was currying the horses and said he'd never seen so much fuss over nothing, but when I picked up a currycomb to help him, he sent me upstairs to sweep out the threshing floor—"In case the day turns bad and they have to shelter the buggies," he said, but I knew he meant so he wouldn't be shamed in front of the company any more than Mam. While I swept it out, I couldn't help thinking one grown-up was as bad as another. Mam kept the girls rushing around all day, cooking and fussing to get food ready. All she gave us for supper was cold potato pie, early at that so we'd have time to get ready before the company came.

All of us had taken our turns in the tub and were dressed in our Sunday best by the time the first buggy turned into the lane. Mam had put on the dark dress she saved for church and her best cap, and the girls were in matching dresses they'd made that spring out of some stuff in a plum color that Mam said was pretty and bright without being flashy. They were made the same way, with fluffy sleeves tight below the elbow and the bodice bloused and gathered at the waist.

Someone seeing them now might think they looked fancy, but they were plain as could be compared to the dresses I saw women wearing in Lancaster, with decorated skirts yards and yards around the bottom and tucks and ribbons and frills and trains that draggled on the ground behind them till Pap said they were enough to put the street cleaners out of business. The girls looked nice, if Mam did have to tease Martha some because she said she'd as soon go to bed early and not bother with the party. But Mammy talked her into getting ready, saying she could go upstairs and lie down whenever she starting feeling over tired. I grinned to myself at what Hen would have muttered hearing that, but he'd hitched up the buggy and gone to fetch Annie Keene and didn't get back till the party was under way.

Ella Leaman and Frank Denlinger were the first to show up. I could tell Barbie was relieved that they came early, because they were neighbors, and she and Ella had gone through school together. Ella lived beyond the railroad tracks towards Paradise, and Frank's people had a farm just this side of the Gap that I always liked because they had a big martin house on a high pole in the meadow where the Newport Road turns off the Pike, or they did till a few years ago when a storm blew it down.

Barbie rushed outside to grab Ella's hand and help her down from the buggy. Of course I got sent to show Frank where to take the buggy up behind the barn and help him unhitch. By the time he was taken care of, buggies were coming up the rise beside the barn every time I turned around, so it wasn't long till I felt as sweated as some of those horses.

I was glad when Sam showed up, grinning as usual, and helped me with the last of them. He wasn't invited any more than I was, but we knew Barb and Hen wouldn't mind the two of us hanging around. We'd both done enough to earn our way by the time we'd unhitched a dozen buggies and finally had a chance to walk back to the house with our cousin Dave and see how the party was getting on.

Dave was in a good mood and joshed us that we were at home tonight instead of over at Paradise getting religion from the strange preacher. He was wiry like Biney and not too big with eyes that always made him look half asleep. But Dave was lively enough, so Mam said sometimes that the energy Uncle Elias and Aunt Annie should have had must somehow have got siphoned off into him and Biney. We asked him why he put us to the bother of unhitching his horse when he could have walked the half mile from Uncle Elias's. "Women do that to you," he said, looking droll and winking. We knew he meant he'd had to use the buggy to fetch his girlfriend.

"Now if anyone should have walked, it's Biney," Dave

went on, "as much fuss as she made about having a ride over here tonight, when she must have walked it a half dozen times today, carrying dishes and checking on things." We all laughed at that, and I could tell Sam was as set as I was on watching how she got along with Amos Landis, who she'd pestered Barb into setting her up with, and as ready as I was to tease the life out of her tomorrow. At the house Dave ducked into the kitchen to say hello to Mammy and Pap and went right on into the front room to find his girl. Stopping at the door, he looked back at Sam and me and said, "Well, come along if you're coming," so Sam and I scooted after him and into the thick of it.

It seemed like there were wall-to-wall people, so that even with the front room and the parlor both open, I could see why they called a party like this a crush. I knew just about everyone, at least to recognize, if all of them were older than Sam and me, though it threw me a bit to see them all squeezed together in two rooms in our house and all gussied up in their fanciest clothes. Most of the girls had on dresses something like Barbie's and Martha's, bright and puffy on top but with plain skirts short enough that you could see their shoes.

Right off I noticed one girl who was dressed different, wearing a fancy skirt with stripes on it and so long it swept against the floor. She couldn't have been much older than I was, and she was small and thin with the kind of face that looks to be all mouth and eyes, especially with the dark hair puffed around her face. As soon as I saw a chance to ask who she was, I poked Dave, and he said I should remember, because I'd seen her often enough before she grew up so much and stopped wearing braids. "That's Minnie Hoffman," he said, "the fresh air girl from New York the Leamans get every year." I asked who she'd come with, and Frank told me Barbie had fixed up for Bill Rohrer to fetch her so she wouldn't be alone at the party. With that he turned away. I decided I'd keep an eye on Minnie Hoffman, but just then Sam grabbed my arm and dragged me into the parlor.

Barbie was there, chatting in the middle of a bunch of people, and Martha was sitting by herself at one end of the horsehair sofa. We went over and asked her if she'd like some company, but she turned her head away and said she was perfectly all right as she was, so Sam plunked down beside her, and I perched on the arm of the sofa where I could reach a bowl of popcorn on the parlor table. "Who's Barbie's new beau?" Sam asked, pointing with his chin. "You know Barbie doesn't have a beau," Martha snapped back, while all three of us stared at Barbie and the fellow she was talking with, Biney half blocking our view where she was rolling her eyes at Amos Landis, who was studying his feet and looking like he was contemplating whether he should invent a new little shuffle dance. "Then who's that Barb's talking to?" I asked Martha. "I didn't unhitch his horse, or I'd remember a face like that."

"I don't see anything wrong with his face," Martha said, "if it does look nicer than some I could mention." Sam and I stared all the harder at the strange fellow, who must have been around twenty. I have to admit he wasn't ugly, if he did have the kind of face I don't much like, all sort of flat and pudgy with a chin that looked to use up half of it. "He looks like a missionary," Sam said, and I said, "Who is he, Moss?" After a minute she said his name was Willis Shirk and he was a friend Amos Landis had brought along. At that Sam and I started to laugh. "You mean Biney came with two fellows?" Sam asked. Even Martha smiled, though she told me to hush up when I exploded that if Biney came with two young men, she had two to drive her home and might as well have walked to the party, for all the lovemaking it would get her. I was still laughing when Martha said "Shush!" and Barbie walked over with Willis Shirk, saying she especially wanted him to know her sister.

Sam and I lit away from the sofa, but I looked back from the parlor door to see that he'd sat down beside Martha. The two of them were looking prim and taking each other's measure, so I figured they might be a match. Barbie had gone off to talk to someone else.

Back in the front room, I looked to see where Minnie Hoffman, the New York girl was, and then sort of edged towards her, Sam right beside me and the both of us pretending all we wanted was general company, though Sam knew better and I knew better, and each one knew what the other was about. We hadn't half gotten there when Annie Musser stepped in front of me. Sam grinned and ducked away, while Annie Musser planted herself like she had a root to China and said she was so surprised and disappointed that Enos Barge wasn't at Barbie's party.

Annie was the sort to worry you once she'd taken a grip, and she wasn't about to let me loose till she'd gotten what she wanted. When I pretended to look surprised and said, gee, I guessed Enos wasn't here at that, she fussed at me about what a nice couple he and Barbie made—didn't I think so?—and how much Enos liked my sister—which I'd certainly noticed, hadn't I?—and what a shame it was they'd had a disagreement—and did I know what it was about?

I didn't know Annie very well, because she lived a good piece away at Witmer Station and went to church at Mellinger's, though her young man was from Paradise, and she was second cousin to Frank Denlinger. And I never have much liked being fussed at. I've noticed since that the people who know you least are most likely to do that to you. Just then I felt like reaching out and hitting her one or, failing that, speaking up and telling her to mind her own business so I could get on to Minnie Hoffman.

Instead I looked at my feet and grunted yes or no when I had to and clenched my fists behind my back, because I figured what went on between Barbie and Enos was none of her business. Even worse, while I was stuck there, Sam gave a grin so wide it almost cut his face in half and moved beside the New York girl where she was standing with some others. So while Annie Musser cross-examined me, I wasn't concentrating too hard on her questions and hardly even knew what she was saying, at least not till she smiled and thanked me and said she just wanted to know about Barbie and Enos so she could finish setting up rides for her party next week. I'd been a real help, she said, before she turned her back real quick, while I was still trying to think where I'd grunted while she blabbed and to figure out what help I could have been, since I didn't remember that I'd said anything at all. I made sure to give her a dirty look before I took off towards Sam and the New York girl.

She was a lively one, you could tell. Maybe it was her dress and the fluffy way she had her hair when the rest had theirs mostly smoothed back from their faces, but she seemed different from the other girls at the party, though I didn't know how different right away, not till she started talking. When I finally got close enough to get a good look at her, she was standing beside Ella Leaman and listening to Frank Denlinger and Bill Rohrer talking about the Democratic Convention that had ended the week before in Chicago and how the anarchists were taking over the country. Even at best, our people never have thought much of Democrats. As for what they were trying to put across in that 1896 election, we could hardly believe what we'd been reading in *The New Era*. What with the parties splitting apart and the communists and socialists taking over the convention, none of us would have been surprised if the country had flown apart and ended in a big bang practically any minute.

Frank Denlinger was just saying that if they put the dollar on silver we might as well all pull up stakes and move to Canada. "Everyone knows a silver dollar is only worth fifty-three cents," he said. "If they shift the standard, everything else will get measured the same way. Those anarchists are trying to ruin us and pull down the country."

I'd been paying attention to what Frank was saying but keeping an eye on Minnie Hoffman, too, and she'd started to look sort of funny while Frank was talking. She wasn't smiling, and she'd opened her mouth a couple times like she wanted to say something. By now she was glaring at him so hard he noticed. "How can you be so stupid?" she said, and it was like she'd spit the words, mad as she was.

Frank hadn't been watching her to know she was mad, and he looked so surprised I started to laugh, till she glared at me, too, and stamped her foot. "You're all stupid," she said, as if she was taking in the whole county. Poor Frank didn't know what was going on, because Minnie was his girlfriend's guest and special friend. All he could tell was that somehow or other he'd put his foot in it. He was so surprised that he just stood there, trying to figure out what was wrong and not knowing how he'd tramped on her toes any more than the rest of us did.

Ella was surprised, too, but she had the sense to ask what was wrong. Minnie Hoffman didn't take long to tell us. "You think you know so much," she said, "when you've never even thought about the country or about anything outside your own little farms." I could see Sam was itching to jump in and give her what for, but Frank noticed too and signaled him to let Minnie have her say. She gave it to us, all right. She said all we cared about was the price of tobacco so we'd get high prices and have pianos in our parlors. Bill Rohrer couldn't stand that and said we'd be better off to use tobacco for currency than silver, but that made Minnie all the madder.

"Haven't you ever thought about anybody but yourselves?" she asked, her face pale and looking more than ever like it was all eyes and mouth. "Your fields are still here, your cows are still giving milk, you're still eating. But in the cities people are out of work because there aren't any jobs. The Democrats want free silver so it will make prices lower and people can afford to buy things, and the factories will open, and people will have jobs again!"

She'd really gotten herself worked up by then. Everybody in the room had stopped talking to look over and try to hear what the fuss was about. Minnie must have realized all of a sudden that she was shouting and everyone was staring at her, because she stopped, stood with her mouth half open, and then started to bawl. Ella put her arm around her, gave us all a look that as much as said nobody should say any more, and herded Minnie through the knots of young people and out into the porch.

As soon as she was gone we all looked at each other and Bill Rohrer gave a whistle. "She's a hot one," he said. "Maybe," Frank said slowly, "but maybe she has some cause. Her father worked in an umbrella factory, and he's been out of work for three months. Ella's people had to pay the fare so she could visit this year." He looked thoughtful till Sam asked if that meant Frank was voting Democratic. Frank didn't think it was much of a joke and said seeing things from a different angle should make you think about where you stood, but Bill Rohrer laughed and said it would take more than a city girl throwing a temper tantrum to change any ideas around here, knowing what free silver would do. "It would stand us on our heads so nothing would be the same," he said.

By then people were back laughing and talking. Sam and I moved around, watching how the girls looked at their fellows and spying on Biney whenever we got the chance. She was still jabbering away a mile a minute and batting her lashes like she had a speck in her eye whenever Amos Landis looked up from the new dance he was working out on the carpet. Sam and I poked each other, because hard as Biney was trying to make an impression, the one we got was that Amos was too shy to know what to do or say, even if Biney had slowed down enough for him to get a word in edgewise.

After a bit I noticed that Ella and Minnie had come back inside, and Minnie was smiling at Bill Rohrer, so I guessed Ella had managed to calm her down out on the porch. Some people had started to sing, too, after Ella and Frank started them on "Ben Bolt." They were halfway through "When You and I Were Young" when I noticed things had got quiet again, except for Ella and Frank finishing up the chorus. People were sort of glancing towards the porch door and trying to act like they weren't staring, so I got up from Pap's Morris chair where I was resting my feet and looked around to see why.

Hen had finally shown up. He was standing just inside the door with Annie Keene hanging on his arm. Annie's hair was done in a knot, but it was the kind that didn't stay where it was put, and the first thing you noticed was all that reddish gold floating around her face and gleaming in the lamp light. She was wearing a frilly white dress with a skirt to the floor, and I could tell right away every fellow in the room was staring at her as if she'd just stepped off the stage at the Fulton Opera House. When they got to the end of the chorus, Frank and Ella stopped singing, and the whole room was quiet, everybody staring and nobody knowing what to do any more than if Annie Keene had stepped into the party from the moon.

Annie and Hen stood there like they were posing for all those eyes to take a photograph, Hen with his mouth straight and a frown, and Annie looking like she didn't care about anything, her cheeks redder than I remembered and a smile I'd have thought was as bold as I ever saw, except that years later she told me how scared she was and what a front she put on walking into that party. Them standing there, it was as if everyone in the room had got frozen solid, and for the life of them, nobody could talk or move till my cousin Dave shouted, "Hi, Hen!" Like that was a signal, everybody took a breath, and the talking and moving started up again. Sam ducked through the people and went over to say hello, and I followed him, wanting to get a closer view of Annie Keene.

Barbie had been in the parlor when Hen came in, but she must have been watching for when he'd show up, because before I got across the room she'd struck her head out of the parlor door and called, "Hey, everyone, Hen's here!"

I knew Barbie had mixed feelings about Annie, even if she had given Hen the letter, but she thought as much of Hen as he did of her, and she had written out an invitation especially for Annie when he asked her to. It didn't take a wink for her to hurry over and shake Annie's hand, saying how glad she was she'd come to the party, then turn around and introduce her to the people nearby. I saw some people turn their backs and step out of the way, but Frank and Ella said hello and introduced her to Minnie, and Biney came bustling out of the parlor, Amos Landis straggling behind her. In a couple minutes Annie and Hen were in the middle of the party, everybody bunched around them, talking and laughing louder than before.

A little earlier Mammy had stepped in from the kitchen to say we could eat whenever we wanted, and now people were walking around with plates in their hands filled with Mam's bread and Pap's ham and all the cakes and pies the women had gotten ready. The front door was pretty busy, too, with fellows stepping outside whenever they had the chance. Sam and I knew what that was about, because some of the fellows were likely to have bottles they could take a nip from now and again, so we ducked out too, making sure we were close to Dave while the bottles made the rounds.

We were both feeling like we were floating when the singing started again, only it wasn't "Ben Bolt" this time. One of the fellows started shouting out "Bill Bailey," and everybody joined in. After that it was "I Don't Care." Sam and I decided we might be missing something, and when Dave screwed the cap on his bottle and stepped inside, we hurried after him in time to hear Minnie Hoffman saying she had a new one she didn't know if we'd heard yet. She was standing beside Annie Keene, though if I hadn't been so tall I wouldn't have known, the fellows were so bunched up around the two of them, Hen and Bill Rohrer on either side.

Minnie started to sing:

> A sweet Tuxedo girl you see,
> Queen of swell society,
> Fond of fun as fond can be,
> When it's on the strict Q.T.
> I'm not too young, I'm not too old,
> Not too timid, not too bold,
> Just the kind you'd like to hold,
> Just the kind for sport I'm told.

All the fellows boomed in for the chorus and shouted out "Ta-Ra-Ra-Boom-de-Aye" so loud it seemed like the walls were shaking. Not many of the girls were singing but mostly were looking on from the outside of the ring around Annie and Minnie. I saw Barbie standing in a corner with a funny look on her face. Some of the others were looking on as if they didn't know what to make of it any more than Barbie, but others were huddled and talking in bunches at the edges of the room, loud, so they could hear each other over the noise. I heard someone say, "It's downright immoral," and someone else say, "I don't know how she has the nerve to make such a show of herself." "It's that Annie Keene," another girl said. "Bold as she is, she's sure to spoil any party."

Sam and I walked past as if we hadn't heard, listening to hear Minnie sing the rest over all the jabber, because the second verse sounded to be as good as the first one. Minnie had just gotten to "Boys declare I'm just immense" when I heard my pap's voice. He was standing in the kitchen door, and wasn't smiling. "Better hitch up if you want to get to church in the morning," he called over Minnie's song. Minnie stopped in the middle of a line, her eyes big and looking surprised. Annie Musser and some of the other girls kept on talking like they were too good to listen to anyone and didn't expect that my pap might be looking on to make sure things didn't get out of hand. "It's almost midnight," Pap said loud as before. Annie Musser and the girls around her finally shut up, and Pap said, "Silas, Sam, you'd better go out and help these young people hitch up so they can get on home." We knew that was an order, whether we liked it or not.

Pap knew what he was about. Sam and I had barely gotten up the barn hill when fellows started streaming out after us. "I didn't know it was so late," Amos Landis said, so worried that Sam and I figured he wouldn't waste much time dropping off Biney. Dave said his girl's people would be fit to be tied if he didn't get her home pronto, and Bill

Rohrer said it was a pity the old man had to break up a good party. Very shortly a string of buggies was easing down the barn hill, stopping at the house to pick up the girls, and heading out the lane towards home. When the last one was hitched up, Sam rubbed his forehead and said he'd better hit the sack. I knew what he meant and didn't stop to watch him head off towards Uncle Menno's.

When I got inside, Mam and Pap and Barbie were in the kitchen waiting for me. "Martha went up an hour ago," Mammy said while she turned down the lamp wick. "I'll just leave on the light till Hen gets home." "Do you think it went all right?" Barbie asked at the stair door. "Well as could be expected," Pap said, and Mammy sighed. "Young people nowadays are so wild," she said. "Now Barbara," Pap said, putting his arm around her. "Don't forget that we were young once."

"I thought the party was fine," I whispered to Barbie on the landing. "I'm glad you did, Sike," she answered, "but I wish I knew for sure."

At church the next day I heard that Amos Wenger hadn't gotten any converts at his Saturday night preaching and was asking where all the young people had been. From what I gathered he wasn't too happy to hear they'd been enjoying themselves at our house instead of listening to him talking about the end of the world at the Paradise Church.

XII.

Word around church next day was that Barbie had given a wild party, though it spread in the kind of whispers that buzz underneath the regular talk and don't always get to the person most concerned. Barb and Mammy had both stayed home to clean up after the party and get ready for my brother Bob and his family coming for dinner, so neither of them heard what was being said, and if Martha did, she didn't open her mouth about it. From the looks he gave me once or twice when I started to talk at dinner, I suspect that Pap picked up some of it, and maybe Bob too. He teased Barbie some about parties and beaux, but not enough that she could tell there was more talk than usual about what the young people were up to.

But as soon as we finished and the women were busy redding up, Bob's Galen hauled me off to a corner of the porch and wanted to know all about the party and whether it had been as wild as some people were saying. Of course I described it all to him and maybe even spiced it up some when I saw his eyes getting round. Smart as that kid was, I didn't often get the chance to show him that being his uncle, I knew a sight more than he did.

Still, we got over the party all right, if Mammy did run on about the kinds of songs young people sang nowadays. Or we thought we'd got over it, till Tuesday, when Barb came back from Esbenshade's carrying a note in her hand and wearing a face like the sky before a hail storm. We could tell she was fit to be tied, though we couldn't tell why right away, seeing that what she had was an invitation to Annie Musser's party the next Saturday. I knew she'd been happy enough when Annie told her she was having one and wanted her and Biney to come to it, and Martha too, till Martha said a night drive that far would be too much for her health, though she thanked Annie kindly for the thought.

But Barb and Biney clacked like a pair of geese at the idea of going as far away as Witmer where they were likely to see some new young people. I remember them talking about the fellows who might be there, laughing and giggling while they ticked them off. So I knew Barb had been as excited as Biney about that party—until she got the invitation and found out Annie had arranged for her to go with Enos Barge.

I couldn't help remembering the night I'd seen them when Barb ran into the house bawling and Enos tore up the lane whipping his horse like he'd forgot all about how proud he always was of driving a good one and treating it right. I'd never seen a fellow crazy mad like that, and it stayed with me. Enos had stopped showing up at Paradise meetings, and I hadn't seen him since that night except once when Sam and I were in Strasburg and he went by in the buggy. I spotted him right away because the horse he had was black with a white blaze, but when he got close enough to recognize us he pretended he didn't, just kept his face dead ahead and gave a cut to the horse till I thought the buggy was going to lift off the street, fast as he went by.

So I remembered that fierceness in Enos, but I remembered something else, too, from when he'd called to her through the dark sounding as much like a little kid as Barbie did sometimes, and reminding me of the way I felt the time the gobbler penned me in the brooder house when I was little and I couldn't get out till Mam came and chased him away. But maybe I've added that part since because I'm old enough to understand a lot more than I could then. I don't remember that I felt sorry for Enos that summer, but knowing what it's like to want something bad, I do now, and for Barbie, too, acting like a little kid who has to make Christmas dinner when she doesn't know how to set the table. I think she was remembering that fierceness in Enos too and was scared, because she didn't know how much he'd want from her once she was beside him in the buggy.

But Mam wasn't feeling sorry for either of them. Barb screwed up her face like she was going to cry and said, "I just can't go with him, Mam," while Mammy wiped her hands on her apron and ran her eyes over the invitation before she said she didn't see anything wrong with going to Annie's party with a nice young man like Enos. "You'll have to settle on a man one of these days," Mammy said, "and you could do a lot worse." "Oh, Mam!" Barbie said, then grabbed back the invitation and ran upstairs.

Barbie fussed and fretted all week, but as usual, work went on. After the party Mam had me haul the quilting frame back to the front room where the women could work on Barbie's quilt when they had time, and through the day Pap had us all out hoeing tobacco. It would be another two weeks before it was ready to be topped, so he didn't object when Mammy said the huckleberries should be ripe and it would be a shame not to take time for picking.

Mammy did love to pick berries. She had a row of currants in the garden, but what she especially liked was getting out somewhere, because she and Pap both liked to visit the woods and wild places. Pap knew the names of all kinds of plants and what to use them for, but Mam loved to head for a berry patch and fill one kettle after another, as if getting her arms scratched and itching from wood ticks was the biggest pleasure of her life.

I think about huckleberries now sometimes, when they serve those big shipped blueberries: enough like them that you know they're cousins but so different that one bite and you remember how wild and sweet the old kind were. Eating the cultivated kind over my cornflakes, I always remember what it used to be like, out getting a stiff back from bending low to pick enough for a kettleful. I haven't been out for years to look if they're still growing.

Mam always seemed to know when they'd be ripe and made sure she dropped little hints at just the right time so Pap would scratch his head and say a huckleberry pie would taste good about then, and Mam would agree and mention that the wineberries were out, too, and she needed them to mix with her currants for pies and jelly. Sometimes Pap teased a bit. Huckleberries only grew to amount to anything in the Welsh Mountains, and he might say he didn't know if he could spare horses for an expedition that far, but he always ended by saying if Mam thought a bunch of hard little berries was more important than cultivating his crops, he guessed he'd have to rethink. Often enough he went along, because you didn't send women even to the lower slopes of the mountains where the berries grew without a man to keep an eye on them and make sure none of the hill people came around. No one knew what those people might do if they found our women alone in the bushes, and no one risked finding out.

That year I remember how smug I felt when Pap said he had to run the wagon over to Abram Souder's for some repairs but he guessed I was man enough to drive the women to the mountains and look after them. That made me feel pretty good, if Mam did shake her head and say, "Well, at least he's tall enough." Martha said she'd as soon stay home, and Hen was off to see about a school he'd heard about near the Monument. Barbie ran across the meadow to ask if Biney wanted to go along, and I hitched Bluebell and Star to the surrey while Mammy scrambled together kettles and buckets and sunbonnets, happy as could be, humming to herself. Before he rumbled out the lane, Pap called back, "Be sure to say hello to Sarah and the baby!" He'd known all along that Mam had in mind a visit at Sarah's, and the huckleberries were only half the reason she had her mind set on a drive to the mountains.

It was exciting to get near the mountains, sprawled out in front of us like a big black spider stretching its legs across the yellow and green fields that rolled right up to the trees and stopped. I think Barb and Biney and Mam and I all held our breaths when the road left the fields and plunged into the trees. The horses hesitated, too, maybe because of the shade but partly because the road was uphill now, and they felt the weight of the carriage the way they didn't in the valley.

Once there we didn't lose any time. Mam made a special point of telling me to be sure and stay near. "Mission or no mission, they haven't made the mountains safe yet," she said. Before I knew it she'd filled her kettle while mine was still half empty. Biney and Barb weren't picking too fast, either, the two of them off a bit and talking low to each other, so I guess Barb had Annie Musser's party on her mind and was talking it over with Biney. Biney must have been taking something seriously for a change, because I didn't hear any whoops or giggles, just low talk far enough away that I couldn't tell what they were saying.

It wasn't long before Mammy put her kettle in the carriage and took a new one to go after the wineberries growing in a prickly stand against the woods. Wineberries were bigger and a lot easier to pick, so I went with her, happy to be reaching up and out instead of stooping myself into a pretzel over the huckleberry bushes. As I figured it, Biney and Barb were both built closer to the ground so it wasn't so hard for them, but given my choice, I'd risk scatches instead of a backache. I liked wineberries, too, red like raspberries but clear so the light shining through made them glow in the sun. We were soon out of sight of the girls, but I figured it was all right, knowing they were close and them being together, and Mammy forgot everything once she had a kettle hanging from her arm and a berry bush in front of her.

She'd almost filled her kettle, and I was making some progress on mine when we heard Barbie scream. Mam was on the other side of the bushes from me. She swiveled her head each way, looking to see how she could get across. I could see how scared her face was when she said, "Run, Silas!" as though she didn't have the wind to shout it. And I did, the wire bail bouncing on my arm and the berries hopping up and down in the kettle while I loped around bushes back to where the girls were.

I heard them before I saw them, talking with someone and laughing some so I knew to slow down before I came on them and didn't come galloping up like a fool, since I could tell they knew whoever they were with, even before I came around a clump of bushes and saw them standing with Ella Leaman and the New York girl, Minnie Hoffman.

That wasn't strange. Lots of people came after berries, and it was a day for it, only we'd gotten an early start and hadn't heard anyone drive up. Mam came puffing up right behind me, scratches on her arms where they showed below her sleeves and a couple rips in her dress, so I figured she must have come straight through the wineberry patch. She looked pretty mad, too, when she saw nothing was wrong. Barbie looked surprised, as if she couldn't figure out why Mammy was in such a frazzle. "What was all that screeching about?" Mam said, still so upset I could tell she'd have given Barb what for if Ella and Minnie hadn't been there.

It must have struck Barbie all of a sudden what Mam had thought and why she was so upset. She looked at Mammy's scratched arms like she wanted to cry and said she was sorry. "I didn't mean to scare you," she said, "but Ella and Min came up on us so, and they startled me." I could see Mam was still ready to light into her, but Biney and Ella saw, too, and they both started chattering at once, Biney saying she almost screamed, too, and Ella apologizing for not calling out to give a warning that she and Min were there. I kept my mouth shut, trying to look like I was above such foolishness and watching from the corner of my eye to see if Minnie Hoffman was noticing me.

If she was, she didn't give any signs and hardly said any more than I did while Mammy and the other three kept up a gabble. I don't know if Mam remembered that Minnie was the one doing the singing on Saturday, but from the way Minnie held back and kept her head down, I guessed Ella had explained to her what my folks must have thought, hearing a song like that. Hard as I tried I couldn't catch her eye, so after five or ten minutes I cleared my throat to make my voice sound as much like Pap's as I could and said if we wanted to stop at Sarah's it was time we were getting on. Mammy sighed, maybe because she was catching her breath after the running, and said she figured I was right and we had enough berries anyway. "Oh," Barbie said. "I spilled mine with the fright." Mam clicked her tongue and said how careless young people were, so I could tell she was back to herself again, while the girls scrambled to pick up Barbie's berries and scoop them back into her kettle.

It was a bustle and a clatter, with Mam stopping to chat with Ella's mam and brother, and more general gabble, before she and the girls and the kettles all finally got loaded in the surrey. Then we were off, Bluebell and Star stepping lively till we were off that mountain, both so nervous and jittery that I had to go easy on the brake till we burst into the fields and sunlight. The team calmed down then, Mam sat back in the seat, and Biney started chattering more nonsense from the back, all of us relieved and happy to be in the sun where we felt comfortable again. Soon Mam was reminding me where to make the turnoff and I was grumbling back that I knew perfectly well where it was, and then we were at Sarah's.

I never much liked their place at Weaverland, the Dan Wanner farm. It had good meadow land right beside the Conestoga, but the house always looked bald to me, too white and stark, maybe because it was covered with white frame and hardly had any trees around it because Sarah's John said trees could shelter too many pests. I know it never looked as good to me as old Peter Eby's place where they used to farm down by the Gap. That house was thick stone under the stucco and solid and sheltered, not stuck bare on a rise like it couldn't relax and had to keep an eye peeled in every direction.

Sarah's guinea hens scattered when we drove in and called out in high-pitched giggles that sounded as if they were having fits, and we saw John's sister at the door looking to see who it was. "It's your mam, " she called inside in Dutch before she came out to welcome us. I realized when I got older what a handsome woman she was, if she just looked old to me then, maybe thirty-five or thirty-six with a wide mouth and calm eyes under heavy dark hair. Her eyes looked half dreamy, and you knew right off nothing could ruffle her, even having her pap not forgive her for marrying Toby Denlinger when he couldn't talk Dutch. Her doing that was enough to show she was all Eby and did what she liked. One thing for sure, with her there, Mam hadn't any reason to worry about Sarah not being looked after.

Inside in the kitchen we found Sarah in a rocking chair nursing the baby while her next youngest played on the floor with a wooden spoon. Sarah fastened her dress when we came in, and Mam hugged her and scooped up the baby, cradling him and touching his face while she asked Sarah one question after another and cooed over how beautiful he was. I remember Sarah laughing while she answered and finally saying, "Well, it wasn't easy, but look what I have to show for it." Mammy sighed then and waited till John's sister went to the summer kitchen after some cookies before she launched into more questons to find out, without asking right out, if Sarah was being looked after all right. "Fine, Mammy, fine," Sarah said, till she noticed how disappointed Mam looked. I started to titter till Sarah caught my eye. "Well," she said to Mam, "good as she is, it's not like having you here." Mammy beamed down at the baby and gave him happy little pats on the behind. Barbie had to hold him then, while Mam picked up the other one and settled into another rocker with him on her lap, and I stood and shuffled my feet for fear Barb would pass the baby to me next. I noticed Biney was hanging back as if she wasn't too anxious, either.

The other kids came running in then and swarmed over Mam till she looked like little kids were coming out her ears, and Barbie asked where Peter was and said she couldn't visit without seeing him. Sarah said he was out with his pap and sent one of the others to fetch him so he wouldn't miss Grandma and Aunt Barbie.

By then John's sister had brought in a plate of sugar cookies and Ellie, Sarah's oldest, was helping her pour glasses of cold spearmint tea, so I figured I was safe from holding the baby as long as I could keep my hands full eating. Meantime Mam was finding out for certain how long John's sister could stay and making sure her man was coming to fetch her Saturday afternoon. "Then I'll have Pap drive me over Saturday evening," Mam said firmly. Barb was fussing over the baby, but she looked up at that, her eyes wide like she was scared. "Mam, let me come!" she said, and she said it so panicky we all stared.

"I can look after the baby, and I can help Sarah and make the meals," Barbie said, her words running out so fast they almost somersaulted over each other. "I know how to cook, and I know how to change the baby and wash clothes. I can do it, Mammy, I know I can. Please let me come!" Barbie's voice was usually light and happy, but till she finished her say it was so tight and shrill it sounded like Sarah's guinea hens. We all stopped chewing our cookies and looked at her, and the baby started to cry.

"Ach, Barbie, give that baby to me," Mam said, settling the other against the side of the rocker so her arms were free for the little one. Without a word Barbie handed the baby to Mam, who shushed and patted while his wail swelled through the room and then died away. I took a gulp of tea, and Barbie hung her head. "I'm sorry I made the baby cry," she said, tears standing in her eyes. "Sarah, I just wish I could come over here instead of going to that party. I got invited with Enos Barge, and I'd do anything instead of going."

Sarah and Mam both smiled at that, and Barbie caught herself and half laughed too. "Oh, you know what I mean," she said. "I didn't mean it like it sounded. I'd really like to come here and help and be with you and the baby," but while she said it tears started running down her cheeks. She reached up to wipe them and then flopped on a rug, her head against Sarah's lap. Sarah leaned forward and put an arm around her shoulder, smoothing Barbie's head with her other hand like she was calming one of her little ones. "Is Enos so terrible?" she asked.

"No," Barbie said, hiding her face. "But I have such a bad feeling about going to the party. I know it's silly, but I'm scared." Sarah kept on patting Barbie's hair the way Mam had patted the baby. Biney had gone out with John's sister for more tea, and Mam was only paying what attention she could spare from the rest of the brood, so I felt like a peeping Tom, pretending to concentrate on the cookies while Barbie pushed herself back on her knees and wiped her eyes. "I guess I'm acting like a kid," she said.

"We all do sometimes," Sarah answered, and Barbie sighed. "It makes sense, too," Sarah went on, "since you don't like Enos and want to keep out of his way."

"I never said I didn't like him," Barbie said, but Sarah kept on like she hadn't heard and said, "Sometimes we don't want to do things because they're not right. And the best we can do then is keep away, especially if we have some particular reason."

"I don't have any particular reason," Barb said slowly. "Sarah, it's just this feeling I have."

"How far do feelings get you?" Sarah asked.

Barbie was quiet for a minute before she stood up and said she guessed she wouldn't be enough help to Sarah anyway if she did come, and Sarah said no one could help like Mam no matter how good they were. Just then young Peter came bursting through the door, and there was more bustle while he got hugged, and Barb and Mam both gave him a good looking over to see that he'd gotten over being sick and was as good as ever. He was hefty for a six-year-old and so full of energy that I couldn't see that they'd had anything to worry about, but women always did. Most people didn't lose any except new babies and the ones born silent, but there wasn't much doctors could do in those days if sickness hit. Barb seemed to forget her own frets while she carried on about him, teasing and feeling his muscle to see if it was bigger than last time she saw him, but Mam put her hand over her eyes and was quiet for a minute, so I knew she was thinking about my little sisters and saying a prayer.

Then Mam set the little boy on the floor, stood up, and handed the baby to John's sister, who'd come back with another pitcher of tea, Biney after her. We had to get back if she was to keep her men from going without their supper, she said, and Hen and Pap would be looking for us. Finally the pack of women got loaded in the carriage again, and we headed towards home, Sarah and the kids all calling and waving goodbye while the guinea hens shrieked and cackled till we couldn't hear them any more.

The rest of that week was busier than the first part, what with the visiting preacher making his rounds and another mission meeting Thursday night. Martha was the only one who wanted to go to that one, but of course I had to drive her over and sit through another round of talks about the heathen and hear Amos Wenger again, if it wasn't the heathen in the Welsh Mountains he was talking about. He preached the next night, too, at Amos Leaman's house where they invited people over to listen, but lucky for me Martha wasn't up to going out two nights straight, and I got to stay home from that one.

Sam went, though, because his sister wanted to know what was going on. He told me that Wenger really let out the stops that night, saying nothing could save us if we died before we got converted and ranting on about the state of young people who went to wild parties and wouldn't take time to turn to their Savior. Sam and I both laughed some, especially when I asked if old Peter Eby had shown up to give any testimonials.

Meantime, Barb was jumpy as a cat and ready to cry if you said boo. Friday, I remember, she was so bad with a cow she was milking that Mam said any daughter of hers that couldn't even milk a cow might as well move to Lancaster and set up for a lady. When Barb slammed down the milk bucket and started to bawl, I could see Mam felt bad, but before she could say anything else, Barb ran out of the barn and didn't show up again for a couple hours. I found out later she'd run across the meadow to Uncle Elias's and sat with Grandmother. I never have been able to figure out what that was about, though I've made pictures of it in my head often enough: Barbie sitting in Pap's chair all dark and pretty, and old Grandmother white and scratching out coals on the sheet while Mrs. Divet shuffled around in the background.

Barb didn't say anything about it Saturday, when we were all in a bustle. Mam was getting ready to go over to Sarah's, packing her traveling bag with what she'd need and stopping every half minute to add to the basket of food she was getting ready besides. "Can you spare a ham, with butchering only a couple months away?" she'd ask Pap, and Pap would grunt, knowing full well Mam was going to take one no matter what he said. "It's not like Sarah's John doesn't have hams of his own," I heard him say once, but he let Mam pack away all she wanted.

She spent enough time telling us what to do while she'd be gone, too. Martha was supposed to cook, and Barb was to look to the outdoor things, and Hen and I were supposed to do all we usually did and lots more besides, if I did tell Mammy flat out there was no way I was helping with the dishes and that kind of women's work. "You'll do your father's chores, then," she said, "at least for the night." Pap was to come back Sunday afternoon, after they'd all gone to church and had dinner together. I didn't especially like Mammy and Pap going off and leaving us on our own, but there wasn't much I could do about it, like it or not. They took off Saturday night after an early supper, Mam calling back halfway down the lane to remind us of what we shouldn't forget till she got home again. "Bring in enough wood for the cookstove, Silas!" she shouted last thing before she and Pap turned onto the road.

Hen said, "She'll never change," Martha smiled, and Barbie turned and went towards the house. "Guess I got to get ready," she said. "Come on now," Hen said. "I'm going to a party at the Gap, and I got to get ready too, but I'll let you use the tub first." Knowing how anxious Hen always was to be with Annie Keene, I thought Barb would smile and appreciate the favor, but instead she muttered something about not being in any hurry and left Hen looking after her and scratching his head.

Barb took her bath first, in the wash house where we set the tub up in the summer, and Hen and Martha went next. So I was last and still in the tub and mother naked when I heard a buggy coming up the lane. I sloshed my back pretty fast and grabbed a towel, because funny as Barb had been lately, I wanted to see how she'd act when she saw Enos. I remember shivering when my feet hit the dirt floor and rubbing down in a hurry while I scrambled to the window, keeping back so Enos or anyone else wouldn't see me without any clothes on.

He'd come up the lane and wheeled his horse so the buggy was opposite the kitchen door. Enos didn't get down. In fact, he didn't even look towards the house, just sat there face forward and holding in his horse while it stamped and snorted. I hadn't seen this one before and took a good look, because it was a fine one, high spirited and itching to go.

While I watched I heard Barbie open the kitchen door. She must have stood on the porch a minute, though Enos kept his eyes ahead like he didn't see her. Then I saw her walk down the steps, acting like she didn't see Enos either. When she got to the bottom I heard her say, "Little key, you stay there till I come home," and she bent over and put it under the bottom step in a kind of hollow place we had there. I thought she spent a lot of time at it before she finally turned around and walked out to the buggy. Enos waited till she'd got around to the other side, then leaned over and handed her in. It wasn't cold, but I saw him tucking a blanket around her legs before he flicked the reins and went whipping down the lane. I watched till they were out of sight, not knowing I wouldn't see either of them again.

XIII.

I don't know how long I'd been asleep when the pounding started. It must have been going on for a spell, because it had worked its way into a dream I was having, where I was at the blacksmith's. I was holding a horseshoe with my hands while he pounded. I remember I couldn't feel any heat, but each time, the hammer came closer to my fingers. He was just ready to heave it again when I woke up. Martha was leaning over the bed shaking me. "Wake up, Silas," she was saying. "Someone's at the door." I pushed back the sheet and sat up, still more asleep than awake and wondering who would come visiting at that hour. "You got to see who's at the door," Martha said. The moon was just past full and made the room bright enough that I could see she was scared. I started to say Hen should see to it, but the other side of the bed was empty. He wasn't back yet from his party with Annie Keene.

The pounding kept on, in bursts now, and in between I

could hear someone shouting my name and Hen's and Martha's. "Go down and see who's at the door," Martha said again, standing barefoot in her nightie and all white in the moonlight. While I swung my legs over the bed and scrambled into my overalls Martha didn't even think to turn her back. "Something's wrong," she said. "Something must be terribly wrong." Still tucking in my nightshirt and hitching my arms into my overall straps I ran to the landing and took the steps three at a time, Martha trying to keep up but feeling her way step by step behind me.

I was across the kitchen and had gotten the key from the nail before she caught up and grabbed my arm. "Don't unlock the door till you know who's there," she said, clawing at my arm like a scared cat. "For cripe's sake, Moss," I said, trying to shake her loose. "Who's there?" she called, still hanging onto my arm. "It's Elias's Dave," a voice shouted back through the door. "For God's sake, open the door!" Martha let go of me, but I'd barely turned the bolt before Dave pushed the door open. Behind him I could see the yard and the fields milky and strange in the moonlight, but standing in the door he looked like a shadow so I couldn't recognize him right away. "Dave?" I asked, my voice cracking the way it hadn't been used to for a time. "There's been an accident," he said.

The rest of the night was worse than my dream, because Dave said Barbie was dead. Martha had turned up the kitchen lamp, but I liked seeing Dave's face less than hearing him like a shadow. His eyes and mouth looked limp, and as soon as the light came on he fell into a chair and hid his face while Martha and I stared. "Barbie's been killed by a train," he said, tears running down his cheeks. I'd never seen a man cry before, and I guess my mouth was hanging open. I might have stared all night except for hearing a plop and seeing Martha on the floor in a white pile. She looked dead, too, except that I didn't believe what Dave had said.

"What'll I do?" I said to him, but he didn't pay any attention, so I got down on the floor and put Martha's head on my lap, running my hand over her hair the way I'd do with an animal that was sick. "It's all right, Moss. It's all right," I said, but when she started to make sounds and come to herself, I knew it wasn't.

Dave was still sitting with his face covered when I lifted Martha into a chair. "Say it again," she said to him, and Dave looked up and said, "Barbie was killed on the way home from Annie Musser's party." Martha stared at him across the light, so I could tell she didn't believe him any more than I did, unless we did and couldn't let ourselves know it.

"Where's Hen?" Dave said, and all I could do was stutter that he wasn't home yet. Dave let out a curse and said, "Someone has to go over to Sarah's and let your folks know." He rubbed his hand across his eyes like he wasn't awake either, then got up and walked to the door. "I got to go home and hitch up," he said. "Someone has to tell your folks, but I was hoping Hen would be home to do it." Martha and I sat at the table and watched him walk onto the porch, neither of us thinking to shut the door he left standing open, just sitting while he stood for a minute against the moonlight before he crossed the porch and walked down the steps.

It seemed like we sat for hours, not moving, but maybe it was only minutes. I just know that when the preachers talk about eternity and say how it's forever and the twinkling of an eye, I think of that night, sitting beside Martha and staring at the lamp in the center of the table. Seems as though we could be sitting there still, all of fifty, seventy-five years later, except that one of the cats rubbed against my leg. It saw the light, I guess. The barn cats always wanted in. I jumped up like I'd been hit by lightning before I knew what it was. "Put out the cat, Silas, and shut the door," Martha said. Then she bowed her head and put her hands over her face while tears ran out between her fingers and dripped onto the oilcloth.

I did what she said, but once I got up I couldn't sit down again any more than if my legs had strings on them someone was twitching and moving back and forth, back and forth across the kitchen. "Oh, Sike, can't you be quiet?" Martha moaned, and then I heard the sound I was making, a funny kind of bleat that surprised me, because I didn't know I was doing it till she said that. I gulped and stood still. In the quiet I could hear a horse's trot and the rattle of a buggy up the lane. "It's Hen," Martha said. "Dear Lord, how will we tell him?"

It turned out we didn't have to, because Frank Denlinger had already. What had happened was that just before midnight the young people had started to hitch up and leave for home from Annie Musser's. John Musser's place was on the Old Road just this side of where the Witmer Road comes out. To get home most of them had to go east and get across the railroad tracks some place or other. At least the ones from down our way had to, and there was a string of them, one taking off after another. Amos Landis and Biney took off the same time as Barbie and Enos, with Frank Denlinger and Ella Leaman behind them and Minnie Hoffman and Bill Rohrer next in line.

They talked some about which way they should go, because the Bird-in-Hand crossing had a bad name. Only last January two mules got killed, the men in the wagon just missing it. The crossing scared people, because the tracks curved behind a rise just before they crossed the road, so you couldn't see if anything was coming. Instead, you stopped and listened for the engineer to whistle and let you know if a train was on its way from the West, but before they went across most people said a little prayer that if one was coming, the engineer would remember and do his job. There was a route you could take around that the fellows talked about using, but the girls spoke up and said late as it was they shouldn't waste any time. The bunch of them decided to go straight down the Old Road and cross the tracks at Bird-in-Hand.

Biney and Amos left Musser's with Barbie and Enos right behind, the four of them laughing and chattering back and forth while they trotted down the road. About at Smoketown Enos called that slow as Amos's horse was, he bet his could beat it any day, or night. So Amos whipped up while Biney giggled and hung onto her shawl. They moved along a bit between Smoketown and Bird-in-Hand, but Biney said no one could call it a race, and when she and Amos got to the tracks, he pulled up and stopped to listen for a train. When he didn't hear anything they crossed the tracks, and Amos called for Enos to come on.

He and Biney looked back. The same time, they heard a whistle and saw a train coming around the curve. Enos's buggy was right on the tracks, the horse rearing and Enos leaning hard, fighting him. Barbie was standing up on the side nearest the train. Biney said she looked like she was ready to jump out. Then there was a thud and a crash and a wheeze, and then the sound of the train brakes and nothing to see but a line of cars moving across the tracks, each taking longer and longer to pass. Then the road was empty except for splinters of wood lying all over the crossing.

Amos said he handed the reins to Biney, jumped out of the buggy, and ran back towards the tracks. The train had stopped a ways up, and soldiers were piling out of it and running back towards the crossing. Before he knew it they were all around him, swarming like ants and shouting to each other. "Here's the horse!" one of them shouted, and looking over, Amos saw a dark pile east of the crossing. "The fellow's here!" another shouted. The swarm of figures all seemed to move at once, and Amos found himself running with them to where they were bunched around something lying on the ground. He couldn't push through the circle, but he heard the moans and a shout from another soldier further up the tracks, "His arm's up here! Train must have sheared it off!"

All the time, he said, the moans were so awful he thought he might pass out, and he stood stupid and dumb while the soldiers scrambled all around him. Then he saw some figures in black, Frank Denlinger and Bill Rohrer looking white and scared, and another one walking back and forth in an engineer's cap, wringing his hands and saying "Oh my God, oh my God."

Some of the people who lived near the tracks were round by then, and a bunch who'd come running from the hotel. "Fetch Doc Miller!" one of them shouted to a boy still tucking in his shirt. "Carry him to the hotel!" the same one shouted again. Like clockwork, the inside ring of soldiers bent down, and the outer one opened to let them walk away carrying something Frank and Bill and Amos couldn't see, if they could hear the moans wrenching out of it.

Frank turned to one of the soldiers and asked, "Where's the girl? There was a girl in the buggy," and the soldier called to the others, "Look for a girl. There was a girl, too," and the soldiers went swarming down the track like an army of ants. All they found were pieces of her, cut up and broken like bits of bread they had to gather up in baskets and carry to the station house. The doctor came to look after Enos at the hotel and went along with him to the hospital in Lancaster on the two-twenty train. The accident was at twelve-fifteen.

The fellows didn't stay around. There was nothing they could do, and they had to get the girls home, all of them in such a state that there wasn't much choice. And someone had to tell the families. Biney was to let us know, but Frank knew that Hen was at a party in the Gap, and after he dropped off Ella he went over to see if it was still going on, found Hen, and told what happened.

When Hen came in the door that night, he looked the same as always except for his mouth. It had lines around it and was stretched down at the corners like something had happened to set it in a funny shape, sort of like he'd been cutting ice from the pond in January and his leg got sawed off, and his mouth got twisted from the sound he made seeing it disappear into the water. He kept his face turned away while he said, "I guess you heard." Martha gave a sob and I nodded.

Talking out of that funny mouth, Hen said, "We got lots to do." I stuttered that Dave was telling the family, and Hen looked at me real sharp. "Has he gone up to Sarah's?" I said he'd been by and had hoped Hen would be home to do it. Hen clamped his teeth like he was locking in a string of cusses. "If Mam and Pap aren't back by morning I'll fetch them," he said. "Meantime we have to get ready." He went into the front room and got a tablet and pencil out of the secretary drawer. Then he sat down by the lamp. "We have to think what all needs to be done," he said, staring at the paper.

Mammy and Pap drove home before eight next morning, but even hearing Barbie was dead wasn't so bad as seeing Mam. Pap seemed numb and stood with his hands tucked under his arms, looking as if he'd shrunk over night. But Mammy moaned and cried as if the hurts to the flesh that Barbie couldn't feel any more had got transferred into her. It was all we could do to get her upstairs and into bed, and Pap sent me first thing to fetch Doc Leaman. When he came, he stayed upstairs a long time and said she was having fits and might not live. We should keep the blinds down and pretend everything was all right, he told us, but Mammy knew better.

Martha and Pap sat with her first till her moans got quieter from the doctor's medicine taking hold, Pap sitting by the bed squeezing her hand and Martha scuttling to keep the compresses cold until my aunts arrived. Aunt Mary took over then, but Aunt Sue insisted she had to do the nursing. All day she flitted in and out of Mam's room, hovering over the bed like a moth and saying, "What's that you say?" when anyone tried to ask how Mammy was.

Martha went to bed then, while my aunts looked to things. Sunday or not, they went to work, cleaning and dusting the front rooms and carrying in milk and looking to the household chores. I'll never forget them working that day, because usually they laughed and joked when they came together, even for a funeral, because funerals were for old people you couldn't be sorry had gone home. But this was different, everything quiet except for Mammy's moans from upstairs. When they said anything to each other they whispered, but mostly they just concentrated on what they were doing, stopping now and again to pull out hankies and wipe their eyes. Then Mam would break out louder, and they'd all stop and stare up, then bend over and start to work again. The doctor came back before noon to check on Mam and bring more medicine. When he looked over Martha he said she had the constitution of a horse, but he didn't know whether or not Mam would make it. I almost laughed, wrong as everything was, because I knew Mam was the strong one.

Meantime Hen had worked out a list of what he calculated had to be done and called me along into the parlor while he went over it with Pap. I don't know that I'd ever been in the parlor on a Sunday morning, when it was dusky from the sun being on the other side of the house and felt like a room I'd never been in before, Hen reading out the telegram messages I was to send Lizzie and Mart from the tower at Gordonville and asking Pap if it was all right to get Bachman's in Strasburg to look after the burying.

The whole time Hen was going over things, Pap didn't seem to listen but wandered back and forth while Hen talked, his hands tight under his arms and his head bowed, only answering when Hen looked at him to say, "Is that all right, Pap?" Pap would pause, nod his head, and go back to his walk around the room half as if he didn't know his way around the parlor on a Sunday morning and was looking for something he'd seen there once and forgotten about till he could remember to find it again. "Is that all?" Hen asked when he finished his list. "Have I forgotten anything?"

"The Bible," Pap said, stopping by the parlor table. His hands shook while he pulled the German Bible towards him from where it was lying beside the fancy lamp. From the way he rumpled the table runner I thought for a minute the lamp was going to topple, but he reached out and steadied it. He fiddled with the pages and took a minute to find the center where the family record was written out, the births all fancy in red and black ink and the opposite page empty except for the little girls, Mary and Ellen. Pap stared at the page. "We'll have to fill in the Bible," he said before he turned away and went upstairs to sit with Mammy.

The rest of that day was a muddle and a confusion, so mostly I remember pieces here and there. It was as though I was too surprised to keep track, the way someone must feel when a building collapses on top of him. I think now of the eighteen the tower fell on in the Bible, because it was like I was one of them. The tower had crashed down and I was too stunned from being under the stones to look around and see how the others were getting on, the ones who thought they were safe inside it with me. I remember thinking I was supposed to feel different than I did and wondering how I was supposed to feel and realizing that I didn't know what people felt like when a ton of bricks fell on them. I couldn't tell if I felt anything at all. I hadn't even cried.

Right after church let out Bishop Eby came bursting into the kitchen, then apologized for walking in like that. I remember that seeing him so shaken jolted me, because I knew then that what had happened was real, and the stones from the tower had hit other people, too. When he saw Pap, the bishop stood shaking his hand and squeezing it in both his, his face whiter than I'd ever seen it and his mouth looking like it hadn't any words. He finally asked, "How's Barbara?" and Pap took him upstairs.

I was sitting on the porch steps when he finally left. He stopped when he saw me, half surprised, then patted my shoulder, the same time saying something about trusting in God before he hurried to his carriage. I remember thinking that tall as I was, Bishop Eby didn't often get the chance to pat my shoulder and almost smiling at the kind of joke Barbie would have made—until I turned around and saw Pap at the door. I couldn't tell if he was looking at the bishop driving down the lane or at the fields rolling towards the south ridge. He stood there till the carriage was out of sight. Then he noticed me. He said, "I'll be in the barn," and walked across the yard with his hands tucked tight under his arms, his feet moving like he'd forgotten how to work them and his eyes on the ground.

I found him sitting on a box in one of the horse stalls when Aunt Mary sent me out an hour or so later to tell him they'd brought Barbie home.

XIV.

Pap and Bishop Eby had fixed that the funeral would be Tuesday, and the muddle kept on, so much happening, so many people around, so many things to keep account of, and always the surprise that Barbie wasn't with us to sing and laugh. She was, though, with Mr. Bachman and a man who worked with him in his furniture store. Mr. Bachman came with the box that brought Barbie. The other man arrived later in a wagon with other things, crates of what they needed and a coffin. It was the other man who asked me about ice and sent me down to my brother Enos's where they had an icehouse to bring back a load, then showed me how he wanted it broken to put in the metal box they put the coffin on. I carried buckets of chipped ice up to the house and onto the front porch, but each time I got to the door, Mr. Bachman took them from me and carried them himself into the parlor. I kept trying to see inside, but the blinds were drawn and Mr. Bachman blocked the door.

Dave came over to tell us that Biney was in a state, about what you'd expect from her being there when it happened, and his mam had her hands full between nursing her and answering the questions Grandmother kept sending Mrs. Divet to ask.

Dave brought word from Lancaster, too, that Enos Barge was alive but so bad they didn't expect him to last the night. He was hurt worse than just his arm, Dave said, with bad wounds on his scalp and worse inside that the doctors couldn't do anything to fix. Enos's family was at the hospital, his mam crying and pacing the corridor, but Dave said they wouldn't let her see him. Enos kept calling for Barbie and asking them to bring her to him.

The papers Monday said the same thing, only *The New Era* wrote that Enos thought Barbie was standing by his bed, probably figuring that a ghost thrown in would help circulation, though I don't see why they needed it till they finished describing what Barbie looked like when they found her.

Sam and Hon and Charl walked over Sunday afternoon, hanging back by the gate and waiting till Aunt Mary told me they were there and I went out. They were all acting strange, like I was someone they'd never seen before, and I didn't know what to do till Sam stuck out his arm and shook my hand. "We wanted to tell you we're sorry, Sike," he said, using a deep voice until he choked over my name. Hon and Charl both nodded and stuck out their hands too. "We're sorry," Hon said, but Charl started blubbering when I came to him. "It's so awful," he said.

"We heard they brought her home," Sam said, "and we felt so bad over it we wanted to tell you." I tried to say thank you, but I couldn't and stood there gulping. I must have looked like a fish, trying to say something and not being able to, till Hon spoke up. I think he said what came into his head to get me over it, and what was in his head was the inquest they'd had over Barbie before they brought her home. "Did you hear about it?" Hon asked, and I shook my head. "Well," he said, "they went over what happened and decided it wasn't anybody's fault. The engineer said he blew his whistle before he got to the crossing. All those city men who run things don't know what's going on, so they decided as long as he said he whistled, he wasn't to blame. As if Enos was too dumb to get out from in front of a train if he heard it coming."

"They never asked when he blew it," Sam spoke up, "whether it was in time to warn them or just in time to spook the horse so Enos couldn't move if he wanted to."

"Those city men don't care about things like that," Hon broke in. "All they care about is running things. I'd like to show them a thing or two. They think we're not in politics because we're too dumb, as if it wasn't the church that kept us out. They even think we're too dumb to move out from in front of a train if they bother to warn us it's coming. Some day I'll show them how dumb we are. They said the railroad wasn't responsible." Hon stopped. I'd never seen him look so mad. He turned away and spit in the grass.

"Everybody's saying Enos was racing," Charl said. Quick as a wink Sam whirled on him. "Shut up about that," he snapped. "You know it's not true. If it was, Amos and Biney wouldn't have said they stopped at the tracks. Don't you call them liars." Charl hung his head. It never took much to put him in his place.

"Did you know the train was doing better than fifty-five miles an hour?" Sam asked. All I could do was shake my head and listen while he said that going that fast and coming down a grade, it was a wonder the train got stopped before Leaman Place. I knew it was a special not on the schedule, but Sam said it was a troop train coming back from Lewistown with a load of soldiers.

I don't know why that hit me, that Barbie had been killed by a trainful of soldiers when our people had come to Pennsylvania nearly two hundred years before so we'd never have to fight. But it did. I didn't exactly feel dizzy. It was more like I'd been kicked hard by a cow and laid out on the barn floor. When Charl asked if I'd seen the body yet and if it was true every bone in her body was broken but one in her arm, the pain came. I stared at him, and Sam said, "You little jerk, shut up!"

"We just wanted to say we were sorry," Hon said. Sam grabbed Charl and pushed him through the gate. He looked back from the lane and called, "God bless you, Sike!" The three of them straggled away while I stood with my head up, fighting what I felt. I stayed by the gate till they couldn't see me any more. Then I walked to the grape arbor where the vines kept even the sky out and flopped on the grass and cried.

Looking back, I wonder what I did feel, close as I am now to joining the others, because except for me, they're all gone but Galen and Hon and Biney. The thought of dying still scares me, but what with the world I used to know faded around me, I know better than to be afraid of the change when I'll see Pap and Mammy and the others again. But when Barbie was killed, she and I were young. That was the trouble and why I didn't know what to make of her being taken like that and why I cried and cried under the grape arbor.

But then nobody else knew what to make of it, either. My sister Lizzie and her family arrived from the seashore on the Monday train, all looking like the fanciest pages from the Sears-Roebuck catalogue. Lizzie was a handsome woman, taller than my other sisters and distinguished-looking in her long skirts, but she cried into her lace hankie till her eyes almost swelled shut and it was a relief to have Aunt Mary send her to their place to stay. Sarah came, too. She left all the kids but Ellie and the baby with John's sisters and settled into our spare room, with Ellie sleeping beside Martha in Barbie's place. Sarah was weak from having the baby less than two weeks before and from the ride over, but she was the only one who could stop Mam from moaning through the house, at least while she was with her. I don't remember that Sarah cried much, out loud, anyway.

Pap didn't cry, but he paced, hugging his hands and worrying that Mart wouldn't get home from the West in time for the funeral. I figured he was making himself think of that as a distraction from the thought of Barbie lying in the parlor, but I'm not sure, as much stock as he put on all the family being at funerals.

The rest of us tiptoed in the house, wondering what she looked like and frightened at the idea of what was behind the shut door. I nearly jumped through the roof when Mr. Bachman opened it late Monday and asked if we'd like to see her. I was with Pap in the front room while he read to himself from the English Bible, and I remember the fear that came on me, knowing how broken she'd been and afraid to see. But right away Pap stood up. "Yes, Mr. Bachman," he said, putting down the Bible. "I've been waiting to see my daughter." He walked into the parlor, and I followed him.

They'd set the coffin in the middle of the room. It was the kind they still use up at Weaverland that had two lids, one covering the body and the top part open to show just the head. Mr. Bachman pulled up the parlor blinds, and in the western light we saw Barbie's face in the yellow sunshine. I remember the relief I felt, because Mr. Bachman had fixed her up so she wasn't horrible, even if she'd been so cut and hurt from rolling under the train that no one could recognize her to say it was Barbie when they found her. I started to sob, I was so relieved to see it was her and not something horrible that had gotten into our parlor. Pap stood looking down at her, his arms crossed and his head bowed. "You have to realize, Mr. Hershey, that the muscles relax, and, besides, we had to do a lot of work on her," Mr. Bachman said. Pap looked at her for a long time. Before he turned away he only said, "She should be smiling."

I stayed longer, trying to see. As relieved as I was that she looked like herself, I knew she didn't look like herself, either. Like Pap said, she should have been smiling or pouting or saying something so that the dimples showed. She didn't even look like she was asleep, though the eyes were closed. While I stood looking, I knew that what I was seeing in the yellow light wasn't Barbie at all, only some house she used to live in that could have belonged to anyone, and anything Mr. Bachman had done to fix it up had nothing to do with my sister. She'd left and gone off somewhere. Pap brought Mammy down to see her later, but I was in the barn by then and didn't hear how she carried on until Sarah took her upstairs again and saw her back to bed while Pap went over to Uncle Elias's to see Grandmother.

It was sometime Monday afternoon that Dave come over to tell us Enos Barge had died in the night and about his inquest. They'd had it Monday morning, and it sounded a lot like the one they had over Barbie, only this time the railroad wasn't exonerated from responsibility like it was the day before. Pap asked Dave if that meant they put the blame on the railroad, but Dave shook his head. "They just didn't clear them," he said. "All they did was say the Bird-in-Hand crossing should have a watchman, as if a watchman could look through the hill more than anybody else to see a train that doesn't whistle till it's too late to stop from killing someone." Pap put a hand over his eyes, and I could see his Adam's apple bobbing like he was swallowing hard. "So they murder my child and get out from any blame for it," he said.

Bishop Eby came over Monday, too, to ask if he could do anything and to finish up the arrangements. He'd seen to getting a plot for us in the new graveyard at Hershey's, because the old one where my little sisters were was filled up. Pap took a place for six back from where my grand-daddy Hershey was buried. As the bishop said, that would look after him and Mam and emergencies, and the rest of us could take care of ourselves when we grew up and had families.

Bishop Eby showed Pap the funeral text he'd picked, too, and asked if it was all right. Pap looked it up and sat reading over it for a time before he nodded. It was right to choose Lamentations, he said. He thanked the bishop before he took him upstairs to pray with Mammy. After the bishop left, I remember Pap saying he was glad Ike Eby was looking after things. That was before any of us realized that the text he picked could go any different than we took it.

The funeral was set for one o'clock. Pap wanted it to be at our house, the old way, even if we knew lots of people were likely to be there. Relatives always came to funerals, way too many to fit in the house, and Barbie had lots of friends besides, so it was to be outside in the front yard. Mr. Bachman said he could bring chairs from his furniture store for people to sit on, and Bishop Eby didn't object. He and Abram Brubaker were going to preach. At first Pap shook his head over that and said we should have Jacob Hershey, but he gave in after the bishop said it wouldn't be right to preach over Barbie in German when lots of her friends couldn't understand it.

Tuesday morning we didn't have a good breakfast, Martha looking so tight and pale that I couldn't stand to look at her and Mammy hunched at the bottom of the table. She was over the danger, Doc Leaman said, but she looked more different from herself than Barbie did. Aunt Mary and the others had stayed over Monday to get food ready, but everybody had gone home by then except for Sarah and Ellie. Martha made breakfast, a platter of eggs Mam picked at till her mouth turned into rubber and she'd be crying. One of the worst things I remember was her trying so hard not to be as sorrowful as she was and then breaking into sobs until it seemed like she was blowing her own life into her hankie.

It wasn't easy seeing the others either, Hen like stone and Pap hardly able to sit till he finished fiddling with his eggs, worried because Mart wasn't home yet from the West. It didn't matter that Mart was a thousand miles away in the Dakotas when we sent word Sunday morning, because all Pap could think of was that he had to be with us for Barbie's funeral. I remember Pap wiping his plate with his bread and putting it down again without eating it, then getting up to pace around the room, head bowed and arms tucked in tight, till I pushed back my chair, too, and started out the door. Pap stopped me, saying I should meet the ten o'clock train at Leaman Place in case Mart was on it. He was going over to see Grandmother.

I went out and wandered around, kicking my way to the meadow and sitting on the fence to watch Pap's feeder steers till I figured the train from the West was due, then walking on over towards Leaman Place. When I got there I saw from the station clock that I was almost an hour early, so I walked up and down the platform, my hands tucked under my arms like Pap and my fingers crossed underneath where no one could see them. I said little prayers, too, like, "Please Lord, let Mart be on the train."

When I finally heard the whistle I remembered all of a

sudden that the train came through Bird-in-Hand and wondered if there was blood on the tracks and what people on the train thought when they got there and whether anyone told Mart that's where it happened, because Hen's telegraph message didn't have room for much. And I wondered what I'd say to Mart when I saw him. Mostly, though, I just kept on praying that he'd be on the train and Pap wouldn't be disappointed.

The train blew its whistle a far piece up the tracks, well before it crossed the Pike, so I had time to watch while it slowed down before it finally stopped at the platform, watch it and wonder what it was like when it didn't have time to slow down or blow its whistle. It struck me I wasn't praying any more.

Mart was the first one off the train, jumping onto the platform so fast it was like he'd been snapped off a slingshot and had to run a couple steps before he could get stopped. Then he stood still with his bag in his hand. It was as if he'd used all his energy to get home, and now he was this far, some spring had run down. He stood the way a steer stands after you hit it with a sledgehammer at butchering, that second it's learning it's dead before it falls down. I stood, too, that second. Then I hurried over. Mart reached out and hugged me, his bag digging into my back because he hadn't thought to put it down. We must have stood a full minute before he shoved me back, embarrassed, I guess. He didn't say anything, just looked at me. Mart had always been jollier than Hen, his face more square and solid like his body. He hadn't thought a second about deciding to go out West. It was Hen that thought.

Now he looked as sober as Hen and stared at me, while I shifted my eyes. "It's true," he said, and turned away, his bag hanging stiff in his hand. I waited a bit, letting him get himself together, before I asked about his trunk. "Mr. Stark will send it," he said and turned towards me again. "Let's go home," Mart said. I took his bag from him, and the two of us started down the road, Mart looking around at the fields and ridges like he'd never seen anything like them before and asking about the accident.

Dinner was to be early, and we barely got home in time. Carriages were already gathering on the road. As soon as we crested the rise behind the barn Mart noticed them and asked what that was about. I could only answer that I guessed they must be coming for the funeral. "Before eleven?" he asked. We both stood a minute looking, then made a run for the house.

When we got in the family had sat down, and Martha was ladling out some chicken corn soup Aunt Mary had made. Mart went over to Mammy and hugged her, and Pap and Hen stood up to shake hands. But right away Pap sat down again and bowed his head. Long as it took before he put it up again, I figured he was praying over more than the soup. After that he didn't say much except that it was right Mart had gotten home, if I could tell he was relieved and pleased he'd made it. Pap didn't believe in fussing over what was right to be done.

After we ate, Mart and I scrambled to put on Sunday clothes, dressing together in the room he'd left months before and taking turns splashing ourselves from the washbasin. Mart had pulled the blinds down while we got dressed. That made me nervous, like Mr. Bachman blocking the door to the parlor until he let us see Barbie, the noises, too, like the sounds from the room before we were allowed in. As soon as we were both decent, I headed to the window to look out over the front yard.

Mr. Bachman had set up rows of folding chairs the way he'd promised and all Mam's straight chairs, too, in the front rows closest to the porch where I knew there were others and a Bible stand for the preachers. There was a bare space in front with a trestle where the coffin would rest as soon as Bob and Enos and Hen and Mart and Dave and I carried it out from the parlor. Sam had been standing by to take Mart's place if he hadn't made it back.

The yard looked strange, but I knew enough to expect that. What I didn't expect was to see carriages tied tight beside each other up and down the Strasburg Road as far as I could see in either direction. They were still parking a half mile away at the Blackhorse School, we heard later. And people. Already the yard was filled with them, and more were walking along the road and coming down the lane towards our farm. I don't think I've ever seen so many at once, and all of them talking in low voices, so Mart and I hardly knew there was anything like the crowd till I raised the window blind.

Down in the yard I saw Mr. Bachman running back and forth among the chairs, whispering to people who sat down to find out if they were family, then dashing to the gate and waving his arms. I could hear him calling, "Only family, please! Please, ladies and gentlemen, only relatives inside the fence!" and trying to wave the rest of them into the front field, where they stood in the wheat stubble and trampled Pap's timothy. And more carriages were backed up along the road trying to get to the house. I saw my brother Enos fighting to get up the lane through the people, his wife beside him hugging the baby and the kids in the seat behind looking scared. There were so many people shoving towards the house that they could barely make room to get through, and the horse was skittish. Mart and I took a long look. Then he whistled. "We'd better get downstairs," he said.

In all the years since I've never seen anything to equal it. There were too many people to count, but word afterwards was that more than two thousand showed up. I was glad I didn't have to help with the horses. Hon and Charl had that job, and if it was only for the relatives and the preachers who drove into the lane, they had enough to do.

Downstairs, the house seemed ready to split open from all the relations coming in to say they were sorry and then tiptoeing into the parlor to see Barbie. That's where Mart went too. I got as far as the door, but when I saw Sarah and Mam and Martha sitting together on the sofa, Sarah calm but Martha looking like she was carved out of ice and Mammy crumpled like someone had opened a valve and drained all the life out of her, I turned away and stayed in the front room. Most of the kids had been sent outside to their chairs, but the rest of my brothers and sisters were there, and they made enough to fill up the room, Lizzie especially in a frilled dress that trailed against the floor. I couldn't help thinking how elegant she looked wearing black and dabbing her eyes from a hankie with a matching edge.

"I just wish Pap had let me give some flowers," she said, wiping her eyes with her hankie. "Barbie should have had flowers. It's not as if she'd joined church and wasn't allowed to have them."

Enos raised his head and frowned. Next to Sarah he was the strictest in the family and a lot less willing than she was to stretch his tolerance. It didn't sit well with him to have a sister at the seashore, her husband making his living from rolling people up and down the boardwalk. Enos never had kept back from Lizzie what he thought about her, and he didn't now. "Stop driveling," he said. "If Barbie hadn't joined church yet, she was raised in it and as much a part of it as I am, and she deserves to be buried in it just as if she'd had time to finish growing up and make her commitment."

Lizzie squeezed her hankie and glared at Enos. "What makes you think Barb ever would have joined your stupid church any more than I did?"

Enos was ready to answer, loud, I could tell, when Bob grabbed his arm and asked what the two of them thought they were doing. "Can't you even wait till your sister's in the ground to start fighting each other again?" he said to them. At that Lizzie started sobbing and Enos looked at the rug. "Besides," Bob went on, "Enos is right. Barbie shouldn't have any flowers. She was raised as a child of the church, and it's right she be buried as one."

Just then Mr. Bachman came to tell us they were ready. He was a little man with a mustache who usually acted so calm that I almost laughed to see him, eyes straining and beads of sweat running down his forehead. I guess he'd never had a funeral this big before, because he looked frazzled. I could see his collar was wet and sticking to his neck. Then I realized mine was, too, and swallowed hard while I followed him into the parlor to help carry out the coffin.

Carrying it wasn't hard after we got through the door, if it was awkward being taller than Dave and my brothers and having to stoop. What was hard was getting outside and being in the glare of all those people. All the seats were filled but six for us in the front row. Back behind people were standing solid. I couldn't even see the fence, what with people crowded on both sides of it and more in the lane and the field too, halfway to the road. We set the coffin in front of the porch and took our seats.

Bishop Eby waited a minute before he got up and walked to the preaching stand. He stood a bit longer with his head down before he looked out over the crowd and asked us all to pray. I did, eyes shut tight while what had happened to Barbie swept over me so I was sorry to have to open them when he said amen and to scrunch my face so I wouldn't cry. The preaching was on the text Pap had agreed on, Abram Brubaker first.

For the Lord will not cast off forever:
But though he cause grief, yet will he have compassion according to the multitude of his mercies.
For he doth not afflict willingly nor grieve the children of men.

Abram Brubaker gave a good talk, saying how he used to like seeing Barbie after church, always laughing and making the people around her smile and be happy. He used the text to say Mammy and Pap and the rest of us had God's compassion, even if it didn't seem like it now. We couldn't presume to understand God's way, he said, but we had to believe and know that His mercy was always with us.

But when he sat down and Bishop Eby got up and started talking, I got a funny feeling like the text had been shifted, because the bishop was talking as if Barbie was the one cast off, not us. He said it was a terrible thing to think that any one of us could be cut off and be changed any minute from joy and beauty to something less than clay that people turned their faces from.

He was talking loud, so the people in the field could hear him, but even so it took me a time to realize what he was saying. When I did, I leaned forward and looked over where Mammy and Pap were sitting farther down the row. Mammy had her hands over her face, and Pap had his arm around her trying to keep her quiet. Martha was on the other side, looking straight at the bishop. Her eyes were wide open, and she looked scared to death. The bishop went on to say we should all pray that God wouldn't cut us off before we were ready, just as we should pray for Him to show mercy to Barbie.

It hit me then what Bob and Enos had been talking about in the front room and that they'd been worried over more than flowers. It hadn't occurred to me that it made any difference whether Barbie had joined church or not. Chances were she would have in a few years, but the bishop made it sound important. I sat straight in my chair, sweat rolling down my back like pieces of ice from under the coffin, hardly realizing what went on until everyone was singing. Pap had asked for "Siloam," and if it was the first two verses I used to like, it was the last two I remember from Barbie's funeral:

> By cool Siloam's shady rill
> The lily must decay;
> The rose that blooms beneath the hill
> Must shortly fade away.
>
> And soon, too soon, the wintry hour
> Of man's maturer age
> Will shake the soul with sorrow's pow'r,
> And stormy passion's rage.

Only the people in the front were close enough to hear the pitch and start the singing, thin and shaky through the first lines. That started the ones behind them and then the ones in back in the field till a couple thousand people were singing from the yard and the lane and the field beyond. But the crowd was too big. The ones in back couldn't hear the pitch, and, besides, they picked it up slower than the ones in front. All those voices were singing, but they weren't quite together. It sounded like the song was bouncing around off the farm buildings and echoing back again from the south ridge.

I was glad when the funeral was over and Bishop Eby read Pap's note thanking our friends for kind help and inviting them for supper after we got home from the graveyard. Then Mr. Bachman called the family to stand beside the coffin and opened it for everyone to see my sister's face the last time they ever would. A kind of gasp went through the crowd. The people standing around bunched closer and started talking to each other in voices that made a low hum at first like some kind of machine. Pap had to take Mammy inside, and through the window I could hear her moans over the sound from the crowd.

The rest of us stayed beside the coffin while the relatives got up from their chairs row by row and walked past to look. Lots of people were crying, but the worst part I remember was seeing Biney. One of her married sisters was half carrying her along the line. I'd never seen her like that, crying as if she was out of her wits. She had a hankie over her eyes and stumbled over the grass till her sister got her to the coffin and shook her. Biney lowered the hankie just barely enough to see, then burst out crying worse than before till her sister dragged her on past.

I stayed by the coffin as long as I could stand it, till the family had got by and some of Barbie's friends, Frank Denlinger and Ella Leaman and with her Minnie Hoffman. I remember Willis Shirk coming by, too, and stopping to take Martha's hand and say something to her, but by then the crowd was making enough noise that I couldn't hear what he said. I took it for a half hour or so and then went inside with Hen and Mart and waited with the others while the line of people kept filing past the coffin. I remember Hen glaring out the window and muttering that he hoped they weren't too disappointed at Mr. Bachman's court plaster and paint.

It was almost four o'clock till the procession got started to the graveyard, Barbie in a hearse with glass sides fancier than anything she ever rode in when she was alive. When we got to the little railroad track near Uncle Elias's, I looked back, and all I could see was a line of horses and carriages stretching behind us as far as the Strasburg Road and more turning down after us. I remember passing the tollhouse by the Belmont Road and seeing the toll keeper and his wife and kids standing beside the house, watching us go by and looking to see how many were still to come that he couldn't charge for going through the gate. He lost the toll for three hundred carriages that day.

When we got to Hershey's more people were waiting, so many that Mr. Bachman had trouble making a way so we could carry the coffin to the grave. Over all the voices and crying I could hardly hear Bishop Eby while he finished and said, "Ashes to ashes, dust to dust." It was like that was a signal for the crowd to stop even pretending to whisper. I wanted to cover my ears while I stood by the grave and tried to remember that the creek was still running at the foot of the hill where I couldn't see it for the crowd and the trees. I knew it was rolling through the fields and beside the church, but I couldn't hear it, only a Babel of voices.

XV.

I guess it's a blessing to have so much to do when there's a funeral, all the relatives on hand and the visiting you have to do if you want to or not. Aunt Mary and some of the others stayed home from the burying to be ready when everyone got back, because they knew there was likely to be a swarm afterwards. Maybe it's even good that the harder it is to lose whoever's dead, the more people show up. Even Mammy was pretty good, while she had to be, and even though she didn't eat any of the food, she and my aunts helped the others to.

As for Pap, he seemed to have a satisfaction at knowing Mart and the others were there, not just my brothers and sisters and their families, but cousins a couple times removed we never saw except at funerals. He shook hands hard to let them know it mattered to him that they were eating and visiting with us. He seemed especially glad to see old Peter Eby and stood talking with him a long time.

Meantime, while the family visited, Mr. Bachman and his helper folded up chairs from the lawn and stacked them into his wagon.

The next day we were alone again, only the trampled grass and timothy to remind us how much company we'd had, except for the place in front where the crowd had pushed against the fence so it leaned over half cock-eyed. When I drove back from putting Lizzie and her family on the train to Atlantic City, the house made me think of a coffin, the shutters like lids ready to be closed up over the windows. That was just a crazy idea that hit me, but inside wasn't much different. Hen had gone off to Enos Barge's funeral with Dave, so someone from our family would make a showing, though we didn't know Enos's people, and Martha was by herself in the kitchen, crying. When I came in she said I was to go out and help Pap and Mart with the tobacco as soon as I'd put on my work clothes. While I took off my good things and changed, I could hear Mammy's moans through the bedroom wall and was glad enough to head for the field.

When I got out, Pap and Mart were working their way down rows next to each other, breaking off the tops of the plants so all the strength would go into the bottoms. Mart waved when he saw me coming, but Pap didn't pay any attention till I got up to him. Then he straightened up from the plant he'd just topped, told me to look sharp, and showed me again just where to break off the tender growth on the top so the leaves that were left would grow wide and fat. I felt like saying I knew all that, but Pap looked so strange that I decided not to. When he'd finished explaining and showing me, the way he did every year, he wiped his hands on a piece of bacon speck he had hanging from his waist and sighed. "It's good we have our work to keep us," he said, and looked out over the field for a minute before he moved down the row.

Hen didn't get home from Enos Barge's funeral till past supper time. By then the rest of us had eaten and Martha was washing up. Mammy and Pap had gone into the front room, but Mart and I sat on while he told us what it was like in the Dakotas. "The fields go on and on," he said, "far as you can see all the way to the horizon, with the sky flat against them at the edges."

I asked how big the farms were, and Mart said I wouldn't believe it, but his boss Job Stark had over a thousand acres. He had lots of money, too, Mart said, and a fancy house in St. Louis where he lived winters, but come spring, his wife and daughters left their jewelry in St. Louis and went along out to feed the crew Mr. Stark hired to start putting in wheat as soon as the spring thaw came, because the ground was frozen solid six months of the year. They left the horses in the fields over the winter, Mart said, leaving them to roam free and feed themselves from the hay they left, and come spring they all had long hair they'd grown against the cold, though there were stacks of chaff they could burrow in for blizzards.

Long-haired horses and fields as far as you could see were pretty wild ideas, and I didn't know whether to believe Mart, or if he was pulling my leg the way he used to when he whitewashed a chestnut burr and swore it was a porcupine egg. Still, my eyes must have been big, and I was ready for more, till Martha whipped around from the dishbench and said Mart would do better to be praying for his sister than telling such stories. She was crying, and when she said that I started blubbering too. Putting his head lower and wiping his eyes, Mart said he hadn't forgotten. It was a matter of trying to, he said real quiet. He'd counted on telling Barbie all about the West.

I think we were all three crying when Hen came in, slamming the door and plumping down at the table. Martha wiped her hands and gave a swipe to her eyes before she hustled to the stove and got the supper she'd set back for him. When she spooned it onto his plate he didn't say thank you, just slapped butter on a piece of bread in his left hand, lifted a fork with his right, and shoveled it in, while the three of us stared at him, wanting to know about Enos's funeral and all afraid to ask. Hen emptied his plate before he shoved himself back and looked at us. Touchy as he was at best, we still didn't say anything, but Martha grabbed up his plate and tumbler and silverwear and carried them to the dishbench where she made a show of scrubbing away. I could tell her good ear was cocked to hear what Hen had to say.

Enos's people had a service at their house at noon, but the real funeral had been at two o'clock at the Strasburg meeting house, and even if it was off beyond the other end of the town, lots of carriages and buggies had gone past our place. We all wanted to know about it, but nobody asked till finally Mart said "Well?" and Hen started to talk, slow and quiet at first.

He said the crowd was worse than at our place yesterday. The Strasburg church was fancy, built out of limestone and so big it could seat seven hundred at a time, but Hen said he'd never seen a church so full, people squeezed into the benches and packed into the aisles so it looked like if anyone sneezed half a dozen would come flying out the windows. He said there were at least twice as many again outside, all crowding to get near the church. By the time he and Dave got there you couldn't even hitch your carriage along the road, everything was packed so solid, he said, and all the way into Strasburg, till John Brackbill and some others who lived nearby took rails out of their fences and opened their fields so people would have a place to park. There must have been a thousand carriages and three thousand people, all scrambling and pushing to get close enough to hear the sermon. They were like animals, Hen said.

He was frowning so much that Mart didn't ask right away what the preachers said. We knew that Abram Brubaker had been asked again and Elias Groff that was the Sunday school superintendent over there. When Mart finally came out with it, Hen shook his head and didn't answer for a minute. Then he said that in that mob he couldn't get close enough to hear. "But I don't think it was about Barbie and Enos being in heaven," he said.

Martha had finished washing and thrown out the dishwater. Now she came over to the table and leaned on the back of a chair, so much pain in her face that I looked at Mart, trying not to see her. But his face was funny, too, so surprised and angry that I didn't know where to look next. After bursting out like that, Hen must have taken a look at them too. "Well," he said, more quiet. "That's not exactly the subject of the sermon, I guess. But Groff talked about what can happen if you don't accept Christ while you've got the chance."

Martha turned away. "I think I'll lie down for a minute," she said, and went over to the settee by the door, where she put up her feet and pulled a shawl over herself before she stretched out.

"I heard more, too," Hen said to Mart and me. "People all around are upset over this accident." I guess Mart and I didn't look very surprised. "No wonder," Mart said. "Anyone would have to be a heathen not to be, when the railroad doesn't whistle, and all this happens, and then they get off scot free."

Hen gave Mart a look as if he wasn't any older than I was and said, "It's not that. People are talking about the railroad all right, but that isn't even the beginning of it. People aren't crying over the railroad."

It seemed to me that what people would be crying over would naturally be losing Barbie and Enos, and I guess I said as much, but Hen looked at me like he was a hundred years old. I'd know better when I was older and knew more of people, he said, because when people cried, it was usually for themselves.

"What do you mean, Hen?" Mart asked. Hen told us then about what happened at Mellinger's Sunday afternoon, when the young people at Sunday school who'd heard about the accident at church that morning were crying and sniveling so bad that John Mellinger that was teaching them put aside his text and talked instead about the accident. Those Mellingers knew about everything, John especially, and he knew lots of them had been at Annie Musser's party the night before, because he talked about the lessons they could all learn from what happened.

"What kind of lessons?" Mart asked, same as I was, wondering.

"Can't you guess?" Hen said, talking through his teeth so his mouth hardly moved. "You heard that evangelist that's been around preaching fire and brimstone and that you'll go straight to hell if you haven't squirmed all over church and converted before the world ends. From what he's been preaching, going to a party's enough to damn you, and I guess babies go to hell because they haven't converted and got baptized yet. Anyway, that kind of talk has convinced a lot of people that Barbie and Enos have. That's why people are crying and running to the funerals, because they're scared they'll be damned, too, if they get caught in front of a train and haven't wriggled through a conversion yet."

I'd got scared when I heard Bishop Eby's sermon at Barb's funeral and I'd realized why Lizzie and Enos were arguing, but the whole idea was so wild that it still hadn't sunk in the whole way. Everyone knew you couldn't join church till you were grown-up and ready to commit yourself, and nobody ever bothered to worry what happened if you hadn't, as long as you were raised right.

I wrinkled my nose and squinted at Hen, still not giving full credit to foolishness that sounded wilder than Mart's stories about fields that went on for miles or horses with long hair. Mart and I must have had the same reaction, because we both started to talk the same time, till Hen cut us off, saying he'd spell it out for us. "They're saying Barbie and Enos are in hell because they hadn't joined church yet," he said, "and don't think there aren't people around ready to make hay from it."

Mart and I sat there, both numb. I tried to think of Barbie in hell, flames lapping at her and crying from the pain. But I couldn't. The most that came to me was the way she'd frown when she had the headache or was upset at Hen or Mam treating her like a kid. Then I remembered the way she looked in the coffin, just her body there and her off somewhere else, and I realized I didn't know where she'd gone, if she was in heaven or just asleep somewhere and waiting for the judgment that came when the world ended. All I could tell was she wasn't with us any more.

Hen scraped back his chair. "I'd better tell Pap and Mammy I'm home," he said. While he went into the front room I could hear Martha crying on the settee.

We didn't usually have prayers together in the evening, but a little while after, Pap called the rest of us into the front room and sat down with the Bible on his lap. As soon as we took our places, he started to read John 14. Upset as I was, I remember listening to the words and trying to imagine Barbie in one of those mansions and wondering if a Comforter would come to us. When he finished Pap laid the book on the table, and we all knelt down and prayed. It was a long time before he said amen, but I didn't mind. We were getting up from the kneeling when he said, "Henry, I want you to fill in the Bible."

Hen nodded and carried the English Bible into the kitchen, while I fetched the ink and pens from Pap's secretary. We all crowded around and watched Hen score the page and test the pen tip before he finally set to writing in his schoolteacher's hand opposite her birthdate: Barbara, Killed at Railroad Crossing, July 26, 1896—Aged 18 years, 1 mo. and 3 days.

Pap was leaning over the back of Hen's chair, watching every stroke. As soon as the page was done he nodded. "That's good," he said, then looked up and asked me to fetch the German Bible from the parlor. "When that's filled in, it will be finished," he said.

XVI.

Of course it wasn't finished, much as we all wished it had been. At least the next month kept us busy because of all the work that had to be done on the tobacco. Nowadays they use chemicals to keep down the pests and stop it from suckering, but it wasn't so easy then. A couple weeks after we topped it, we went through and picked off the suckers that tried to sap the strength from the big bottom leaves. We had to do that twice, because any we missed wouldn't cure. We had to keep off worms, too, green things as fat as my thumb with smooth skins and brown warts down their backs and horns on their tails. They were even half pretty, as worms go. The one job I hated year after year was ripping them in half to kill them. If we didn't, they turned into moths as big as humming-birds with eyes on their wings, and farmers didn't like them any more than the worms.

What I mostly remember about working in the fields that

August was that Barbie wasn't with me, because she usually was before. Seemed as though I was always straightening up to tell her something and being surprised again to remember. Mart was with me some and Martha, too, when Mam didn't need her in the house and the weather suited her, but picking worms in particular was my job, if anyone helped me or not, and every time I killed a worm, I thought of Barbie torn up by the train and hated the railroad for doing that to her.

When I think back to what a monkey I was and how I set myself to copy grown-ups, I guess now I must have picked that up from Pap. He was deep, and if doing all that was proper kept him busy, he had time to brood on things once that was done. Pap wasn't about to forget Barbie because all of a sudden she was buried, any more than Mam did. I could hardly sleep nights for her crying, and the flesh on her arms started to hang loose and quiver when she worked. Pap didn't change like Mammy, at least to the sight, but he wasn't the same. He didn't make jokes any more and mostly had his hands tucked under his arms unless he was working on something. His birthday came a week after the accident, but we didn't do any celebrating. I remember him saying, "Next year I'll be sixty."

The four of us, Hen and Mart and Pap and I, were doing our barn chores before breakfast one morning when Pap rested his pitchfork and asked Mart when he was planning to go back out West. Mart shuffled a bit and said he didn't know because the season was getting on some. Then he looked at Pap and said he thought maybe he'd stay home this year, costly as it was to go back and forth.

Pap nodded as much as to say Mart was doing the proper thing. "It's best that you stay home now," he said. He started to work again, then set his fork down harder than before, his face twisted from trying to hold in all he felt. "That engineer," he said, "he should have whistled in time.

The Lord above knows he should have whistled before he came from behind that hill."

Mart and I looked at each other, wondering what we should say. But we didn't have to say anything, because Hen walked over from where he'd been looking after the calves. "I know, Pap," he said. "The railroad killed her, and the railroad should have to pay, but we know the railroad doesn't give a damn. They have the government under their thumb and can get away with whatever they please." He stopped before he added, "If Bryan gets elected, he may cut them down to size."

Pap gave a snort that made me think he was back to normal and snapped out what he thought of that fool Bryan with his silver policy. Hen waited for Pap to get out of his system what was eating him. Mart and I did, too. Pap grumbled away that even that crazy Democrat Marsh at the Gap store knew better than to go along with the wildness Bryan was pushing, wanting to turn the country upside down and bring down our money when, Lord knew, there was little enough of it in our pockets nowadays. "He might as well be an anarchist," Pap said, "but you've got to have a government."

Hen didn't say anything back to Pap, who forked up more before he said, "You know, one thing that's been bothering me is that from what Biney says, Barbie was standing up and saw the train coming. She was standing up, but she stayed in the buggy and let herself be killed. Why didn't she jump out and save herself?"

Hen shook his head. "It probably came too fast," he said, but Pap frowned. "Maybe," he said, "but quick and strong as Barbie was, it wasn't like her."

Thinking about it, it seemed to me that it wasn't like her, either, and I started to wonder what she thought and how she felt, standing up in the buggy and seeing the train come at her, Enos's horse rearing from the fright and him fighting and trying to get off the tracks while the train swooshed towards them.

"It doesn't matter," Hen said, turning away. Pap started to carry his fork to the back aisle. "No, it doesn't matter," he said. "But the train killing her matters, by God!" Mart raised his eyebrows, surprised as I was to hear Pap swear and not realizing any more than I did that the pain he felt for losing Barbie was turned into hate against the railroad. "God damn that engineer," Pap said before he walked out of the barn.

One way or another, everyone else was as upset as Pap, if they showed it different ways. For one thing, Hen started staying home Saturday nights, and when Pap asked if he didn't want the buggy, he shook his head and muttered that he reckoned on working at his books. He'd finally got a school not too far away, at Limeville near the Monument, and said he wanted to be ready come September. A night or so later when we were going to bed, Mart asked him wasn't he seeing Annie anymore, and Hen said he wasn't in much of a mood for good times.

Nobody else was, either. Sam and I were both pretty busy working our paps' tobacco. When we saw each other at church, it seemed like we didn't have anything to say during prayer the way we used to, or after church, either. We were both confused by losing Barbie and by everything else that was happening.

The strange preacher, Amos Wenger, had left the county right after Barbie and Enos got buried, but word was he'd be back. If Barbie's accident was the biggest thing to hit the county until the flu epidemic in 1919, other things were happening to keep people riled, like a city man blown up by dynamite two days after Barbie was killed, and a train wreck just outside Atlantic City Friday the same week because two engineers were racing. Mam broke down and had to go to bed again when we got news of that, moaning and sobbing that if they'd left two days later she'd have lost Lizzie and her family same as she did Barbie. I remember how Pap's face tightened and he muttered about railroad engineers being wild men who didn't care how many people they killed. The preachers talked about all those accidents in their sermons like it was the Old Testament and we were Babylon or Nineveh or Jerusalem in the book of Lamentations.

What they made the most of, though, was the trolley crash outside Marietta just two weeks after the accident. The trolley tracks didn't come to our end of the county till later, but Columbia had got them about four years earlier, and a year or so after, they built a line to Marietta that went along the Susquehanna and climbed up Chickies Hill. Hen went up there once with Annie and spent the afternoon in the park on top, where there was a restaurant and a dance pavilion, and a band from Columbia played music every Sunday.

It was the same one Hen and Annie had been on where the brakes failed and a car went out of control the Sunday after Pap's birthday, running wild down the hill and crashing into a ravine. Six people were killed and almost seventy more were hurt in that accident. The preachers said it was punishment for worldliness. Hen didn't go to church at all after that. I still remember him saying the preachers were too foolish to listen to except that they were so dangerous.

But Martha didn't think they were foolish. At church she sat with her hands folded and her face white, and she stood off to one side after services where she could be by herself. Most people saw she wanted to be alone and let her be, so I was especially surprised a week or so after the accident when Mart and I came in from the fields and saw her in the yard talking to Willis Shirk. Mart nudged my arm, and we took a good look. Martha had her head down and wasn't saying much, and Willis was wagging his chin at her in that way he had. "Looks like Martha has herself a beau," Mart said, but I said even Martha could do better than that. She could have, too, because she was pretty, and she kept her looks for a long time. But there's no accounting for tastes, and the way Martha turned up her nose at all the regular fellows, it shouldn't have surprised me to see her taking up with Willis. Not that they started courting exactly, but after that he dropped by now and again to ask about her, and they'd sit in the parlor sometimes.

I asked Mart once what he thought they were doing there. Mart grinned and said they were probably swapping texts and made me a bet on it, so we sat on the porch steps by the window where we could hear them and look in without Willis seeing us. We didn't care much if Martha did because she couldn't do anything about it with him there. She was so bent on listening, she never even saw us. He was sitting on a straight chair hitched up near the couch, and Mart and I could have stuck our heads in the window and they wouldn't have noticed. From what we could hear, they were talking about baptism and whether you needed it to go to heaven.

"What did I tell you?" Mart whispered to me, but I whispered back that I hadn't heard any texts yet. Sure enough, just then Willis came out with a verse from Mark: "He that believeth and is baptized shall be saved." "Will you believe me now?" Mart asked, poking me in the side, but through the window I heard Martha crying.

When I was fifteen I couldn't understand how Martha could have any interest in Willis Shirk any more than I'd understood what Barbie felt about Enos Barge. Willis came from Drumore below Quarryville and went to church at New Providence, but I'd seen him at mission meetings and that kind of thing. The churches down that way were like the Mellingers, always hell for leather after Sunday schools and missions and raising money to convert the heathen. None of us liked him much, but I guess he was what Martha needed just then. She liked ideas. Years later she'd collar the preachers after church and argue with them over their texts, and when she heard some fly-by-night preacher talking on the radio about predestination, she picked up on that for a while.

But all that started after the accident, with her wondering whether you could be saved without being baptized or whether it did any good if you got it before you were grown up and ready, the way it had always been in our church. Martha sure couldn't get anyone in our family to talk about things like that, so I guess Willis came in handy, even if I thought he was as mealymouthed as anyone I'd ever met. We saw a lot of him that fall, though I have to admit, I never caught Martha as much as holding his hand. I guess that wasn't the way her interest went.

If Martha turned as funny after the accident as if she'd been all Eby, it seemed as if everyone else got funny, too—Mam, Pap, and Hen. And me too, I guess, though for a long time I thought I wasn't reacting at all, except for missing Barbie and remembering and thinking and wondering why she didn't jump from the buggy. It took a time before it came to me that I hated the railroad like Pap and was bitter against the preachers like Hen and was fretting over theology like Martha, but all so deep inside I didn't even know it. If I didn't cry like Mammy, it was because men didn't carry on like that. And Biney did enough of that for both of us.

We didn't see much of her after the accident, though Dave came by pretty often and sat on the steps with Hen to chew over what he'd heard and talk about the chances of finding a farm so he could marry his girlfriend Ella Wilson. I used to think Biney was pretty silly and make faces when I saw her coming, but in the weeks after the accident, a couple times I caught myself hoping it was her when I heard someone coming into the barn or walking up the porch steps. I saw her sitting on the women's side at church, looking as white and scared as Martha, but before services she always scurried right to her bench, and afterwards she squeezed into a huddle of girls so I didn't get to talk to her for weeks after. Seeing the accident the way she did, she took it hard, I knew from Dave and from what Aunt Annie said when she'd come by some evenings. But outside church, I didn't see hide nor hair of Biney.

Bit by bit, I realized I even missed her, and sort of the way I missed Barbie, because the two of them were together so much, giggling and chattering all the time. When I'd look up from what I was doing, thinking to say something to Barbie before I remembered like I did right away, it came to me I was missing Biney, too, and thinking of the two of them. We didn't laugh much any more. Maybe that's what I missed most and why I trotted over to look her up one afternoon after I'd finished suckering the tobacco.

I found her sitting in the back yard snapping beans. She must have heard me coming, but she didn't look up, and I had to stand beside her and almost shout in her ear before she'd even raise her eyes from the kettle. When she did, she looked so bad I wished I'd stayed home, all the jokes and laughs washed out of her face. It looked as if a flood had whipped over her eyes and nose and mouth and left a kind of mess I had to scramble through my mind to recognize.

"How are you?" I asked her, feeling gangly and strange and all of a sudden not knowing what to do with my hands except tuck them under my arms. Biney stared at the pot and kept on snapping beans while she said she was all right, she guessed.

At that I forgot about how I felt, it made me so mad to see her. I said, "For cripe's sake, Biney, you could at least give me a proper hello and not talk to me like I was a visiting missionary." I turned away and stomped towards the back gate, but before I got to it she ran up beside me and grabbed my arm. "Oh, Sike," she said, hanging onto me like I was a tree stump along the Pequea at flood time. I braced myself for what she had to say, but she just said again, "Oh, Sike," and started to bawl.

I wished I hadn't come, even if I hadn't known why I felt so much like seeing her. I know now that I was looking for the part of Barbie that Biney had, too, all that life the two of them seemed so full of. But I miscalculated. Biney was full of life all right, same as usual, but I didn't like this kind.

The way she was carrying on, I didn't know what to do but let her. Being Biney, she made a good job of it, meaning every bit. At first she just bawled and then started hiccuping out how awful it had been and how scared everybody was. All I could do was stand there and wish I was a thousand miles away working the wheat fields with Mr. Stark.

"I keep seeing it," she said when she could talk straight, "and watching it all over again, Enos fighting that skittish horse and the train coming." She covered her face, and it was like I could see it, too. "Biney," I said real quiet. "Did she have time to jump out?"

"Oh, I don't know, Silas. Don't ask me," she said. "Pap asked me and Dave, but how can I tell? It seemed so long, like she was waiting. Maybe she could have if she'd wanted to leave Enos. It all went so fast, how can I tell?"

"You don't know how bad it was," she said then, looking at me like she had a secret she couldn't keep in and at the same time didn't dare tell. I muttered that I guessed I didn't, feeling scared and sick and afraid, because I knew she was going to tell me something terrible, and I knew I was going to listen.

She leaned up towards me like a character in some railway romance and lowered her voice. "The train ripped off all her clothes," she said. "They found her naked. And I saw her. I couldn't even tell it was Barbie, and she just had one stocking on." Biney's eyes were open wide and her eyebrows sort of puckered, making her look half surprised that she'd seen anything so awful, maybe even proud she'd seen something worse than anyone ever saw before. Then she seemed to sag like all of a sudden she didn't have the strength to stand up, and she screwed up her face to cry, quiet this time. "Oh, Silas, I'm so sorry," she said. "I miss her so much, and I keep remembering it."

You better believe I got away from Uncle Elias's as fast as I could, and I didn't look up Biney again. Aunt Annie must have had her hands full looking after that one and Grandmother Hershey besides, because Mrs. Divet was failing pretty bad, till Aunt Annie said she needed as much looking after as Grandmother and she didn't know what she was going to do.

From what I picked up at church, Biney wasn't the only one still having fits about the accident weeks later. All the young people who'd been at Annie Musser's party were in a state, but especially the ones who'd driven home the same way and come through Bird-in-Hand after it happened, in time to see the splinters from the buggy and the horse and Enos propped on the porch of the hotel holding the top part of his arm and moaning and praying. And what was left of Barbie.

Ella Leaman was nearly as upset as Biney, and Minnie Hoffman wasn't much better. She was only supposed to visit for two weeks and then go back to New York, but after the accident she wrote home and got leave from her family to stay as long as the Leamans wanted her. When I saw her at church next time, she looked different. She'd put away her fancy New York dress and was wearing one of Ella's. For some reason, she never looked so good to me after that, hardly as pretty as the other girls and not as nice as Lillie

Denlinger, who edged over real shy to tell me she was sorry and wiped her eyes with a hankie with a frill around it before she slipped back with the other girls, though I could tell she was still looking at me and being sorry.

But if Barbie was with us or not, the tobacco kept growing, and we had to keep working it. The last half of August Pap went out every day to snap the tips of the leaves and test how ripe it was. As soon as it started to make a crackle, he set the shears to the grindstone and said we'd start cutting tomorrow. And we did, shearing off row after row till my hands hurt from working the handles to cut through the stalks.

Come afternoon, when the plants had wilted some and before they had time to burn in the sun, we started the hard work, slipping the spearheads over the laths and threading up the stalks, then loading them onto the wagon Pap had set the frame onto so the laths fitted between, the tobacco hanging down like sets of curtains. It was a lot heavier than curtains, and my back ached till we got it hung. The hardest part was hoisting it into the shed behind the barn, because it sure didn't fly up to the rafters nearest the roof.

I got to stand at the top of the shed, Pap and Hen handing up the laths till I reached down to get them from Mart and lifted them into place. Mam started to cry when she came out with spearmint tea for us and saw me up there, scared I'd fall down, but Pap put his arm around her and said, "Barbara, the boy has to grow up."

After a week of cutting we'd done a loose job of filling the shed and were working at unloading a rack into the barn. It was a hot day, and we were all in a lather when the strange man walked into the barn. Hard as we were working, we mightn't have noticed if the mules hadn't. Ben Gray snorted and stamped at a stranger being there, and Molly whinnied. Pap was just lifting another lath from the wagon when he saw the man. I remember he had the lath half out and set it back down on the rack, gentle, like he was afraid of bruising the leaves. Then he turned around to look at the stranger standing in the light just inside the big barn doors.

"Mr. Hershey?" the man asked. Pap looked at him a minute before he climbed down from the wagon and said yes. The man put out his hand and said, "I'm Ira Winters. I'm here from the railroad." Pap had started to put out his hand, but he whipped it back and wiped it against his overalls. "That so?" Pap said, folding his arms and standing like an Indian at a cigar store. He waited for what the man had to say.

"I've come about the accident," Mr. Winters said, squinting a bit to get used to the dark in the barn while we all stared down at him. "Yes," Pap said, but he didn't say more and he didn't hold out his hand.

Fancy suit or not, I could see that man was nervous, and Pap didn't make things easier for him, standing quiet while the stranger cleared his throat. It was dusky in the barn, and he kept blinking his eyes like he couldn't see right. He said again, "Mr. Hershey, I've come about the accident." Pap still didn't say anything, so the man started talking.

"The railroad is sorry your daughter was killed and would like to do something." He paused, expecting Pap to answer, but Pap didn't. "They'd like to pay you," the man said. "How much?" Pap said then, and the man answered, "They're offering five hundred dollars."

I hadn't seen Pap smile for a month, but he smiled then. The man smiled back, like he was relieved. "Good," he said. "I was hoping we'd see eye to eye." Pap kept looking at him, his hands still tucked in. Then he said, "I'm glad to hear the railroad admits the responsibility of killing my daughter." At that Mr. Winters threw out his hands. "Oh, no, Mr. Hershey. We don't admit anything of the sort. The inquest established that the engineer whistled before he came to the crossing. We admit no responsibility."

"Then why do you want to give me money?" Pap asked, standing so stiff I was afraid he'd splinter to pieces if another word hit him. But the railroad man didn't see that, and he had his answer ready. "It's a matter of good will. We're sorry about the accident, and to show it we're willing to pay you five hundred dollars."

Pap did fly apart then, if he did it in a quiet way that Hen and Mart and I could see and the railroad man was too dumb to. "The train killed my daughter because it didn't whistle in time, and you're trying to buy me off so I'll say it wasn't so," Pap said. "What kind of man are you to think I'll take money for my child's blood?"

The railroad man looked surprised. "Get out of my barn," Pap said. Ben and Molly started to stamp. "Get out!" I shouted from the rafters. The man looked around the barn like he hadn't realized anyone was there but Pap. He backed towards the door looking up into the shadows, but before he disappeared down the barn hill he called back, "Think about our offer, Mr. Hershey!"

As soon as we heard his carriage go down the lane and turn into the road, Pap went into the house. Hen and Mart and I had to hang the rest of the tobacco by ourselves.

XVII.

It was the end of October when the western preacher, Amos Wenger, came back. We'd settled the tobacco in the shed and put the corn in shocks. I remember Martha and me working our way through the cornfield stripping out the ears and tossing them into bushel baskets we carried back and emptied into the corncrib. We brought back the fodder and stacked it against the barn so it would be handy to feed the animals come winter.

In those days, before everybody put up silos, we had a lot of doing to get ready for the cold. Barbie and I always used to work at the corn together, but on a farm you make do with what you have. Martha did well enough, if she didn't cut up the way Barbie always did, so corn picking that year wasn't much fun. Barb would always be singing to herself or passing on some silly story she'd heard or stopping to look at a bird or a rabbit, then working like blue blazes to catch up again.

Martha worked steady, finishing one stalk and picking up the next one, never even stopping when she did talk, and that mostly about the preachers from the West who were coming to save us from our sins. I didn't want to talk about it, so I asked did she mean that fellow Bryan and the election that was coming up. Martha didn't think that was funny.

I didn't think the preachers coming was, either. Bishop Eby had invited them back to lead us by the hand to heaven. Lots of people around, especially the older ones, still thought the best way to get there was the old way, not falling into fits like Paul on the road to Damascus or some kind of Methodist. But Bishop Eby liked to keep up to date. He was real proud of the mission they'd got started at Red Well by the Blue Rocks, though Sarah's John said they'd have to do a lot more Christianizing up there before he'd sell off the guineas or let his hams hang in the smokehouse.

John said you couldn't trust instant Christians, but Bishop Eby didn't care if they were instant or not. Seeing how upset the young people still were over Barbie and Enos, he must have decided it was a good time for making more. He'd kept in touch with Wenger, who'd gone down to Virginia after he left us in July. And Wenger was in touch with all those other preachers who were mixed up together with the Chicago mission and with that new school John S. Coffman had opened in Indiana. Six months before there'd have been too much feeling against all their new ideas for the bishop to have them all in at once, jabbering about how sinful we were going along the way we always had, but things were different now.

The gaggle of them came down on us the last week in October: Wenger again, one named Steiner, and S.F. Coffman that was the son of John S. that had prayed over Grandmother. Bishop Eby talked them up till, from what I heard, half the county was planning on going to the meeting they were having at the Paradise church the last Friday of the month. Martha sure was, if no one else in the family had much stomach for it. All that week Pap hardly said a word more than he had to, and every night I heard Mammy crying in her bed and sometimes Pap talking to her. But I couldn't hear what he was saying.

The missionaries weren't the only excitement that fall. The election had everyone going. Sometimes I think there must have been a fight in heaven that year, messed up as everything was, all the accidents and the changes everyone was trying to make. I remember reading in the paper about a woman who put her little baby in the oven and roasted it to death. That sticks in my mind as the kind of year it was.

I never remember people being so worried about an election or so upset that if Major McKinley didn't win, the whole country would turn topsy-turvy. Some said Bryan's ideas about free trade were enough by themselves to turn the country inside out. No one liked what he said about being sympathetic with the Cubans, either, for fear we'd end up fighting for them. But what upset people the most was that silver plank, his wanting to lower the gold standard to sixteen to one when everywhere else it was thirty.

The Republicans and the Democrats had both already split over that, but there wasn't any split in the county. Tight as money was with the depression and bad market for tobacco, nobody wanted what dollars they had to be worth half what they were before. *The New Era* said the British were behind it, though other times they said it was a plot by the socialists and anarchists. The only one I heard say a good word for Bryan was Hen when he said he might put down the railroads, but even he shut up when Pap asked what would happen to our money. Thinking back, I guess people were so worried to stop that change that they let the one in the church go by, not having energy to concentrate on both at the same time.

Martha was the only one who went to the revival meeting at Paradise that night, and Pap said afterwards he wished she hadn't. At supper she was fidgety and asked the rest of us didn't we want to go, too? Mart laughed and said he might think on it if there weren't a better show going on with the rally for McKinley at Williamstown. She asked me then wasn't I going, and I said Sam and I were going to the election rally, but we'd walk her over if she wanted. "Never mind," she said. "Willis said he'd stop by for me." Pap gave her a look. I don't think he took to Willis Shirk any more than I did, but when Mart asked if she wasn't afraid of catching a chill, Pap said, "That'll do. She'll be all right if that's as much as she catches from those preachers."

Martha always did have a stubborn streak, but she knew better than to talk back to Pap. She set her teeth together before she said she was sorry her brothers didn't care enough about their souls to pass by the rally, but it was their choice. "Probably the right one," Pap said, and Martha didn't say more. Mammy got up quick and started to pick up dishes. "Move your elbow, Silas," she said. It only hit me later that she was as confused as I was what to make of it all. When Martha asked did she want to go along she said she had sewing to do and turned away.

At that Pap thumped the table with his fist. "Martha Ann, if you want to go to that revival meeting and hear your sister set up for an example and racked into more pieces than the train knocked her into, I'll not stop you. But I won't have you worrying your mother." Pap got up and started for the front room, but Hen stopped him. He'd been teaching for the last two months and looked as glum as ever. "Mind if I take the buggy tonight?" Hen asked him. "I think I'll go over and see Annie." At that Martha slammed down a dish, but Pap nodded.

As soon as I could get ready I lit out for Uncle Menno's to pick up Sam and head across to Williamstown where the rally was. Mart probably would have come with me except that Charl and Hon were likely to tag along, and he was too grown-up to hang around with little kids. He asked Hen if he'd give him a lift, and when I took off down the lane he winked and said he'd see me later.

The days were getting short, and it was after dark till I got to Uncle Menno's. My cousin Bess was getting ready to go to the revival, and Aunt Mary was bustling around as usual in the big kitchen while Aunt Sue knitted away in one of the rockers, leaning back and forth so hard I was afraid she'd tip the chair over into the range. Deaf as she was, it wasn't easy explaining to her where we were going, Bess to the revival and us fellows to the rally, but she shook her head and smiled, saying she was sure we'd all help to save the country and we should have a good time.

Dotty as Aunt Sue was, I don't remember once when she wasn't happy to see us and glad we were having a good time. Aunt Mary never seemed to mind having her around, saying another place to set wasn't any trouble, especially when Sue knitted all the socks the boys needed and gave her so much help with the sewing. But that's the way Aunt Mary was, always ready to take on more and never stopping to think over the extra work it gave her. She stopped Charl on our way out because his hair was strubbly, and she straightened Hon's collar, then stood at the door with her hands on her hips to see us out, giving a big sigh that she'd got us started proper and calling out that we shouldn't get into mischief.

The four of us headed across the Belmont Road and out

down the Pike till we got to Williamstown, Sam and me walking fast against the cold and letting the kids tag along behind the best they could. We'd have gone by ourselves except for Hon being so het on going to the rally and Charl having to go wherever the others went. Besides, Aunt Mary said we couldn't go without them.

It was a good walk, over a mile for them and a sight longer for me, but when we got to Jake Bair's hotel where everyone was gathered, we figured it was worth it, with the crowd there and the parade, people carrying torches to light it and showing up from all around, Leacock and Paradise and Harristown and Salisbury and Intercourse and Gap and Bird-in-Hand, all waving their lights and carrying banners to let everyone know they were for McKinley and ready to stop the changes Bryan wanted to make in the country.

I didn't like the speeches so much, bigwigs from the city standing on the hotel porch and talking about how important it was to have sound money and to protect our trade. I leaned over to Sam and said I sure could drink a cold beer, and Sam grinned back and said it was a nice idea if we could find one. "I'm game," Sam said, and headed into the taproom, me behind him and Charl right at my heels, while Hon stayed outside to hear the rest of Mr. Lane's speech.

There was a big crowd in the taproom, too, all the stools filled and people crammed into the booths. The bartender was pretty busy filling mugs and pouring shots, but he wasn't so busy that he didn't have time to look Sam over when he ordered two beers. "Ask your father to get them for you," he said. Sam's face got red and I could see he was mad, but there wasn't much either of us could do about it, so I tugged his arm and said we should look around for Mart, while Charl said we should know better than to ask for beer, anyway. "You'd drink some fast enough if we got it," Sam said, but that wasn't enough to get rid of Charl, and he tagged on after us while we went out again and started looking to see if we could find Mart.

The crowd at that rally was something, people I recognized and lots I didn't because they didn't go to Paradise or Hershey's or to our church at all but were Presbyterians from the Gap or went other places. Funny thing was that there were a fair number of women there, but if I recognized lots of men, I didn't know any of the women or girls to speak of, I guess because all of ours were off at the revival. It crossed my mind to wonder how many of them down the Pike at Paradise were getting saved.

About then we spotted Mart drinking beer with some other fellows and asked if he'd get us some. He said all he needed was the price, so Sam and I dug into our pockets. Sam gave Charl a sip from his a bit later to celebrate Mr. Gatchell saying that no one around here was going to put up with what Bryan had in mind. The cheer from the crowd packed all around the hotel came near to deafening me, and I waved my mug and shouted as loud as anybody.

XVIII.

It turned out we had no worries to speak of about Bryan winning, because McKinley and Hobart swept the country, taking all the East and turning half the South into Republicans for that election. I remember when we got word, Pap saying he wished the other changes he saw coming could be turned back so easy and that the hill ridges would be high enough to keep them out. He was thinking of Martha, I guess, because by the time Mart and I got back from the election rally, she'd got converted.

We heard about it after milking at breakfast the next day when Martha started talking about the revival meeting, saying how wonderful it was and telling us how many had found Christ while her brothers were at that political rally. I gulped over my water glass, but Mammy wanted to know more, and Martha went on talking, her eyes shining like an angel was standing in the middle of the table.

"Brother Steiner preached, but the others were there too,

up on the preachers' bench with Ike Eby. He talked on the Prodigal Son and how we should take the story to heart because it was about us and people who went to parties and political rallies and drank beer when God was waiting for us to come home."

I have to say my heels got itchy when she said that, and I looked around the table to see how the others were taking it. Mart was looking a little nervous, but Hen's face was so red that I thought he might explode like the man killed in the dynamite blast. Mam was leaning over her plate with her eyes so wide I wanted to tell Martha to stop. I didn't, though, and she kept on.

"Then he said we'd sing, and if anyone felt God calling them, they should walk up front and commit themselves so they'd be saved. Everyone sang 'Oh Weary Wanderer, Come Home,' and people started getting up and going to the front. Nettie Hershey was first, and then Frank Denlinger came up from the men's side, and then Cora Ranck and Annie Eby and Ruth Buckwalter. Ella Leaman and Minnie Hoffman went up after them, and then Biney worked her way out the bench, falling over people's feet because she was crying so. She had such trouble that Brother Wenger came down the aisle to get her and lead her to the front bench.

"And then, hardly even knowing what I was doing, I was going up front, too, and before I knew it Brother Steiner was shaking my hand and leading me over to sit beside Biney. He prayed a long prayer, thanking the Lord for the harvest and asked us to stay after the others left so he could talk to us about how glad he was we'd accepted Christ."

Mart whistled. "Sounds like half the county's converted already, and the preachers just got here." Hen jumped in then, biting off his words sharp and hard so I knew how mad he was. "It's hard to believe my own sister would go along with those revivalists," Hen said, and he spit out "revivalists" like it was a swear word. "They're like a bunch of vultures flocking in to feed off the dead, taking advantage of Barbie and Enos being killed and using them to work up every featherbrained girl in the county. It's easy enough to see how they could snare Biney, flighty as she is even when she's not in fits the way she's been since the accident, and the others too, all afraid they'll go to hell because the preachers tell them they will if they haven't joined church before they die."

Hen was leaning forward and talking right at Martha until he was shouting at her. "How could you turn against Barbie like that, Martha Ann Hershey? What you've done is tell everyone that her own sister thinks she was no better than she should have been so they can wring out more converts. Damn you, you think Barbie's in hell, and you get converted so you can be better than she was, as if you were worth her little finger. I can hardly believe that Barbie's own sister would be the first to damn her."

We all knew better than to cross Hen when he was that mad, all but Martha, who was stubborn as he was. "Don't you swear at me, Henry Hershey," she hissed back across the table, glaring at him so her eyes looked like blue marbles. "For all I know Barbie is in hell, because the Bible says it: He that believeth and is baptized shall be saved; but he that believeth not shall be damned. Jesus Christ said that, but you're more interested in taking His name in vain and in running around with that Annie Keene than in reading your Bible, I suppose."

Sarcastic as she said that, I don't think it took. Hen looked at her like she was a cow too dumb to stand still for milking. He didn't answer for a minute. Then he pushed back his chair. "Christ, but you're a stupid bitch," he said. "If it's baptism that makes the difference, Annie will be in heaven before you because she's Presbyterian."

"At least I won't be damned in hell like you, Henry

Hershey!" Martha shouted at him before he slammed out the door. She went pale then, and leaned back and looked at the ceiling, her face drawn and tired. "I had to join," she said. "Something made me and I had to." She turned to Pap, the hardness gone out of her face and looking all of a sudden like she was about six years old and explaining why she'd spilled the cream. "You understand, don't you Pap? I didn't mean to hurt Barbie, but I did what I had to."

Pap had been sitting with his head bowed the whole time Hen and Martha were fighting. Now he looked up, his face more tired looking than Martha's. He gave a nod. "I understand," he said, "if I don't think much of those preachers. But Bishop Eby invited them, so I won't talk against them. Just one thing, Martha, that I want you to keep in mind." Martha said, "Yes, Pap," and he said real quiet and deliberate so I've never forgotten. "That verse says: He that believeth not shall be damned, and your sister believed, if she'd joined church or not."

"Yes, Pap," Martha said real low. Pap got up and went into the front room. Martha turned to Mammy, her face still tight and scared. "Mam, you understand too, don't you?" she asked Mammy, who'd been as quiet as Pap through all the ruckus.

Since Barbie was killed, it was like part of Mam had been broken into as many pieces as Barbie was by the train. I think the hardest part for the rest of us was seeing how she could be the same size and shape and yet look so different. She gave a funny kind of smile when Martha asked that and said maybe we were all looking for something that could lift our guilt, and she wiped her eyes.

I knew what was bothering Mammy. She put the blame on herself for Barbie being killed because she talked her into going to the party with Enos instead of letting her go to Sarah's the way Barbie wanted. Barbie being killed was an accident, the rest of us knew, but Mam couldn't see it that way. She thought she'd murdered her, so that seeing Mam so upset made me think of Christian in *The Pilgrim's Progress* she used to read to us, bent over from the big bundle he carried on his back before he got to the Cross, even if thinking that didn't make sense because Mam had belonged to church for thirty-five years.

I know Pap told her she wasn't to blame, but I still heard her crying and knew she was carrying a guilt that wasn't hers. Maybe that's why she was so interested in what Martha told about the Friday night preaching and at seeing the strangers at Paradise church on Sunday.

Those preachers hit the county like lightning. Besides all the converts they got Friday, they picked up more Saturday, when Wenger preached at a house and snagged Elmer Leaman that was Ella's brother and Aaron Buckwalter. I heard about that at church when he preached again, telling us how we'd fallen away from God. "I've visited with you before," he said, "and my heart ached at the looseness and backsliding I saw. I heard before I got here that there'd been a falling away, but I couldn't credit it till I saw the drinking and looseness and running after worldliness with my own eyes." He said what had happened to Barbie and Enos was a sign like the message to Lot before God destroyed Sodom and Gomorrah, and he told us God was waiting to welcome us if we listened or to send us into flames that would burn us forever if we didn't. Then he prayed out loud, asking God to bring us into the fold and giving thanks for the people who'd already come in. Lots of people were sniveling until he finished. Before church let out they read the names of the converts and gave a list of the places where the Westerners would be preaching next week, so many I couldn't remember them all. I couldn't see how anyone could stomach so much church at once.

It seems I wasn't the only one who felt that way. Mammy hadn't felt much like having people over for Sunday dinner since Barbie got killed, but Pap always thought a lot of old Peter Eby and liked to see him, especially because he lived alone on his farm. When he asked Mam did she mind, she shrugged like nothing mattered any more. Martha had her good ear cocked and asked could Willis Shirk come too, and Mammy shrugged again.

So we had old Peter and young Willis both over after church. It wasn't the likeliest combination, Willis looking so pious in a new official Mennonite suit like the Western preachers wore that you'd have thought he was saved half a dozen times, and Peter the Hermit looking more like a slab of concrete than ever.

Over dinner Pap was polite enough to Willis, if no one talked much to him except Martha. Mammy asked him now and again if he wanted more food and kept passing dishes to him, but she didn't have much talk in her any more. A couple times Mart tried to make jokes, but they might as well have been horse apples dropping onto the table. Hen didn't help either, sitting as grumpy as I ever saw him and not answering with more than a grunt when Mam asked did he want more chow chow or schnitz and knepp. He wasn't about to make himself pleasant to Martha's beau when he blamed Willis for stuffing the religious craziness into Martha's head and Martha for turning against Barbie. Pap and Peter Eby talked some at their end of the table, but all in all we were about as cheerful over dinner as a pen full of hogs at butchering time.

I think we were all glad when we'd finished the pie. Hen went upstairs to work on his lessons, and Mam started stacking the dishes. "You run along and entertain your friend," she said to Martha, but Martha wasn't one to shirk and said he'd be all right till she finished helping Mam redd up. That meant Mart and I were stuck with him. Mart gave me a look and I gave one back to him, and then both at the same time we asked Willis if he'd like to see around the farm. Pap took Peter Eby out, too, to show him how the stock was getting on and how the tobacco was curing.

I have to say, considering that neither of us thought Willis Shirk was worth a skinned rabbit, we did pretty well by him and showed him the two heifers we'd kept to breed and the bull and the horses and the steer stable and the pig sty with the two Poland-China sows and the big barrows ready for butchering. Willis didn't seem very interested, though, and Mart and I took turns telling him more than he ever wanted to know about our farm, while he kept stopping to scrape his feet. Finally there wasn't any more we could show him or tell him about in the barn, so we took him up to the tobacco shed. Mart and I both liked the sharp, strong smell of the tobacco when it was hanging, but Willis's face got red and he started to cough, so we hurried him out again and down below to the stripping room. We knew it smelled just as strong down there, but we didn't know what else to do with him since we'd covered everything else but the manure pile.

The stripping room was built into the stone foundation right next to the damping cellar where we put the tobacco to get it ready to work on. Through the fall and winter we all spent a lot of time there, working at the tables that ran along the walls, so it seemed the natural place to go even on a Sunday. I didn't know that Pap and Peter the Hermit had gone there, too, until we opened the second door and were all but in.

The two of them had pulled stools up by the iron stove Pap had lit to take off the chill and were talking real serious, every now and then taking sips from a couple enamel cups. When we came in Pap looked up and told us to help ourselves to the cider and went on listening to old Peter, who was talking in German about the revivalists but switched to English when we came in out of politeness to Willis.

"They might as well be Baptists," old Peter was saying, "all this *Gemüt* and *Gottseligkeit* and stirring up feelings, as if committing yourself was a clap of lightning. But I'll tell you, I've known men hit by lightning, and if they live through the first jolt of it, they're the same people they were before. If Ike Eby wasn't such a fool, we wouldn't be having all this trouble, turning our young people wild because they don't have enough trust to know they're God's children without going through some conversion."

Old Peter took a sip of cider, but he wasn't finished by a long sight. It always struck me funny that people called him Peter the Hermit when he talked plenty at our house, but I guess he knew Pap had respect for him, and he just didn't bother with people who didn't. Resting his mug on his knee, he went on to say he couldn't see much basis for this idea that people had to wear special clothes to show they were Mennonite, either, as if the Apostle Paul meant a coat with a notched collar and a special dress for women when he told people to put on the armor of holiness. "As if God would damn a man for wearing a necktie," he said.

"But foolish as that is," old Peter went on, "it doesn't go against the rules of the church. These other things they're about, they do. Nobody but Ike Eby would invite those revivalists here and let them have a series of meetings like this when it's written in church rules they're not allowed to."

Mart and I had perched on some boxes by the side table and were sipping cider and listening. Willis hadn't sat down, maybe for fear he'd mess up his fancy suit. After one sniff at the cider he'd set his mug down, too, as if it was a little strong for his insides, but he had his ears perked and was listening to what Peter Eby was saying. Now he spoke up bold as you please, as if any idea of his was just as good as Peter the Hermit could have.

"The rules say you can't have meetings more than once

or twice in a row the same place," Willis said real smart, "and I can't see as any rules are being broken."

Pap and old Peter both looked up sort of surprised, neither of them expecting that if we came in where they were, we'd interrupt what they were saying, but I guess old Peter sized Willis up as being as big a fool as the bishop and decided to let him have his say. "So you don't think so?" he said.

I always thought Willis Shirk had a better opinion of himself than anyone else did, and if I wasn't much interested in anything he had to say, I couldn't help laughing to see him face off to Peter the Hermit, till Mart dug his elbow into my ribs. I shut up then, and pompous as you please, Willis Shirk set old Peter straight.

"Of the three of them, not one is preaching the same place more than once in a row," Willis said like he was teaching mission school to someone from Red Well. "Brother Steiner preached on Friday, and Brother Wenger preached Sunday, and the next place he's preaching is tonight at Strasburg. They're all taking turns at different places, so they're not breaking any rules." Old Peter nodded as if what Willis said was true as the Bible.

"What about the preaching at people's houses?" Pap asked real quiet, "like that Wenger giving a sermon at David Hostetter's last night? Seems to me that all those meetings are in Lancaster County and in the same part of it, if they're not all at the Paradise church."

"You can't say they're breaking the rules, " Willis said, sticking out his big chin and spreading his mouth into a smile so satisfied with himself that I felt like smacking him one.

"No," old Peter said, looking at the mug on his knees, "you can't say they're breaking the rules. Just that they're doing all they can to get around them, the three of them coming instead of one so they can take turns and moving from one church to another and preaching at houses and even getting an invitation from that bunch of church Amish to preach Monday night. No, you can't say they're breaking rules, if all of them preach the same thing, and the same people go to hear them each time. Seems to me they might as well spare the trouble of taking turns and moving around. The pharisees were pretty good at not breaking any rules, either."

Willis's face had gotten red, and he wasn't smiling any more, but old Peter didn't seem inclined to spare his feelings. "Then there's this business about conversions and having to join church to belong to the Lord. That doesn't break any rules either, though we all know it goes clean against all we ever held about baptism, as if young people can only be saved if they've been revived first like a bunch of Methodists. I don't know that this Moody fellow the wildness seems to be coming from is a Mennonite."

Willis looked mad, and I could see he didn't like the dressing down he was getting. He stuck out that chin of his and said, "I think you're wrong, Brother Eby."

Old Peter wasn't ruffled. He nodded and gave a little smile. "Have you thought out where this is going, Willis Shirk?" he asked.

Willis was just waiting for a chance to speak up. "It may be going back to what the Bible tells us," he said, "and away from all the sin and worldliness that's going on around here." Old Peter raised his eyebrows, and Willis looked at the mug on Peter Eby's knee.

Peter the Hermit raised it to his lips and took a sip. "It never crossed my mind before that a mouthful of cider on a Sunday afternoon would go near to damn me," he said, "any more than it ever struck me or anyone else around here that babies and young people who die before they join church don't go straight home to the Lord." He was talking real quiet, but there was an Eby glint in his eye when he said, "Next you'll be telling me we have to have infant baptism to save the souls of the little ones."

Mart and I grinned at each other, because Peter Eby had talked Willis into a corner the way I knew he would, since if there was one thing Mennonites believed, it was that people had to be grown up before being baptized meant anything. Willis knew it, too. Problem was, he wasn't smart enough to follow how old Peter had led him into that corner and didn't know enough to shut up when he was beat.

"The Bible says you have to be baptized to be saved," Willis said, talking too loud and his face redder than ever.

"The Bible says lots of things," old Peter said, quiet as ever, "like 'Suffer little children to come unto Me,' and I don't remember that our Lord said anything about them having to be baptized first." It was like he'd been half-teasing Willis so far, but I could see he was as serious as I'd ever seen him when he wrinkled his eyebrows and said with a kind of kick to the words, "I tell you, you follow out this idea that people have to be converted and baptized before they can get to heaven, and the next thing you'll be a Roman Catholic saying abracadabra over babies and believing in saints and magic."

Even Willis was smart enough to get the point of that, if he was still too dumb to shut his mouth. "That's not so!" he said, and was going to say more when we heard Martha in the entrance way, saying fast and nervous that she thought we might be here.

I'd been so bent on what Willis and old Peter were saying that I hadn't heard her come in, so I don't know how long she'd been by the door listening too. "I thought you might want to go into the house," she said to Willis, giving him a funny look and adding that she'd finished the dishes, as if her being there didn't tell us that without her saying so. Willis turned around and looked at us, as if he was trying to think what he could say for a last shot to make himself look less a fool, and we all looked back at him. What he finally did say was more to his credit than anything else I ever heard him come up with, because he turned to Peter the Hermit, shook his hand, and said, "Thank you for the talk, Mr. Eby," before he followed Martha into the entrance way and we heard the outside door slam. I think we all sighed with the relief of having him gone, and old Peter sat for a minute shaking his head. Then Mart and I poured some more cider and sat back to hear what old Peter had to say about the election.

I suspect that Martha heard a good bit of that conversation between Peter Eby and her beau, because I didn't hear her talk after that about baptism, and she didn't seem so taken with Willis as she was before, as if she didn't trust him the way she had at first after the accident when she seemed to hang onto him to see her through the jolt of it—which isn't to say she didn't hold to what she'd done or stop trying to make the rest of us see the error of our ways and get converted, too.

Mammy was the only one who paid much attention. Hen stomped out of the room when Martha started that kind of talk, and Mart and I teased her till she clenched her hands and said we were no better than the heathen from the Welsh Mountains. As for Pap, he usually pretended not to hear when she got started, though once I remember him saying it might be more profitable for the visiting preachers to convert the railroad than to bother with people like us. The railroad sent letters every couple weeks, saying they were sorry and trying to give Pap money, but he ran his eyes over what they said and put them in his secretary. He didn't answer them but walked around the next couple days with his hands tucked tight under his arms. Whenever

I saw him like that, I swore under my breath at the man who did it.

But Mammy listened when Martha talked about the revivalists. It was the first thing she'd shown any interest in since we'd lost Barbie, so none of us was about to stop her if she wanted to go to the extra meetings, and before I knew it, I found out I was supposed to drive her and Martha to Hershey's for the preaching Tuesday night.

From the time they got there those strangers kept as busy as if they were hauling in wheat against a hail storm. The same Sunday we had Peter Eby and Willis Shirk to dinner, they held an evening meeting at Strasburg where more than a thousand people showed up. I don't know how many converted that night, but on Monday when the applicants all met over at Hershey's in the afternoon, Martha told us there were more than sixty converted and wanting to join church, more young people than she'd ever seen together at the same place even at parties.

I couldn't understand how so many got turned so fast, and most not much older than I was. When I said as much to Martha, she said maybe some young people knew more now than they used to and I was old enough to look to myself. Then she told us all about Preacher Steiner and Preacher Coffman and the talk they gave the applicants.

From what she said, it sounded as if they talked mostly about clothes. Besides the suits they wanted the men to wear, they had special ideas for the women. It wasn't enough that their dresses were plain and not made fancy like the ones Annie Keene or my sister Lizzie wore and that the older ones generally wore a kind of shawl over top and a cap for good. The women had to have special dresses, the preachers said, to show they were set off, and Preacher Coffman especially said Mennonite women all had to wear the same kind of cap and all the time because of what Paul said in Corinthians about it being a shame to a woman not to have her head covered. What our women wore, he said, weren't caps, they were prayer coverings to show that everything they did all the time was a prayer.

Mammy listened to all Martha said, and that Tuesday when she and Martha got me to drive them to Hershey's for the night preaching, I think she got converted, too, if you can do it when you've been a good Christian all your life. Pap stayed home, saying he didn't need any outsiders to scare him into godliness. Mart didn't want to go, and I didn't even ask Hen. I knew Sam was going to be there with Charl and Hon because his sister Bess had pestered him into it, and I figured all the family on the Mellinger side would be there too, interested as they were in preaching, especially if it came from out West, so I didn't figure on being lonely.

Somehow, it wasn't what I expected. Preacher Coffman spoke, the young one. You could tell he was educated and not like the preachers I was used to that were picked by lot and never had training in what to say except what was put in their hearts. This fellow didn't even look Mennonite, wearing his special coat and standing up front so slender and fancy. One look, and you could tell he'd never forked out a steer stable. Sam and I made some remarks when we saw him sitting up on the preachers' platform, but we both shut up when he started to talk.

I don't remember what he said, just how different he was from what I'd seen before. He wasn't exactly good looking but was blond and had a face that was long and sort of rounded, not square like Bishop Eby's, as if all the education he'd had had smoothed off the corners. He was young, too, not more than twenty-three or so. Till he started to talk, I couldn't imagine that he was old enough to be a preacher.

But he could talk, if I'm still not sure it was real preaching. Standing up behind the pulpit, he told us about having faith in Christ. He didn't use his hands or shout or raise his voice, but it was his voice that made the difference, going up and down and punching in the words that counted, always so I could understand but sounding different, like the words were polished and from someplace far away. When he finished I wasn't really surprised to see people get up and walk to the applicants' bench, six of them and all around my age. I looked at Sam, and he made a face at me, but I saw that Charl was crying on the bench beside him. When I looked over to the women's side, I saw that Mam was, too. Her head was bent and she was wiping her eyes with one of her church hankies.

Then everyone started to sing. It was a new song I hadn't heard before, but I could tell the ones who went to singing school had learned it, because all the parts came through so the rest of us could follow along.

'Tis the harvest time, 'tis the harvest time,
To the fields I must away;
For the Master now is calling me,
To go and work today.

Gleaning on the hillside,
Gleaning on the plain,
Working for the Master,
'Mong the golden grain.

'Tis the harvest time, 'tis the harvest time,
Oh! who will go along?
See the fields for harvest now are white;
I hear the reaper's song.

'Tis the harvest time, 'tis the harvest time,
There is work for all today;
If you cannot be a reaper,
You can bear the sheaves away.

I thought the doors and windows would burst open with the sound of it, especially the chorus, the men rumbling the bass and playing against the top part the women were singing. I heard Charl beside Sam singing out as loud as anyone else.

When the service ended and we were all scrambling after our wraps, I saw that everyone looked happy from that song. My cousin Dave who'd come with Ella Wilson leaned over to ask me if I wasn't going to convert like Biney and Martha, but I said being born once was good enough for me. Sam, right beside me, asked Dave why he hadn't gone up to the front bench. "I think I'll wait till I get married," Dave said, "as soon as I find a farm."

If Sam and Dave and I didn't get converted by the strangers, lots of others did. Martha and Biney and most of the ones who'd seen the accident joined at Paradise at the end of the month in a class of thirty-nine, the biggest ever at one time before. Sixteen more joined at Strasburg, twenty-one at the Old Road, twenty at Hershey's, and more yet at New Providence and Willow Street down near where Enos's people lived. More were getting ready, too, like the twenty-nine at Hershey's that weren't as fast as the first bunch. The Western preachers were gone by the time they all got taken into the church, but no one could forget they'd been through, not just because of the young people joining, but because of people like Mam.

The day after that meeting she and Martha walked over to Esbenshade's store. They said they were just going for the mail, but they took their butter and egg money, and when we men came in later, the two of them were cutting out dresses and had a bunch of white net on a chair to make into coverings. Pap gave them a look and asked why they were onto a new project when no one had finished Barbie's quilt, but neither of them wanted to hear about that. "We're making new clothes," Martha said, whipping their stuff off the table and scrambling to set on the plates so we could eat.

"I never knew godliness could be judged by the clothes people wore," Pap said under his breath, but Mam was at the stove dishing up and Martha was too busy putting down knives and forks to pay attention to what he said.

XIX.

If we didn't have more snow in those days than we do now, it stayed longer. What I remember about that winter is mostly snow and grayness, though I may partly be thinking about the new clothes the women made for themselves. They all dressed alike now in sober colors cut out to a pattern they passed around to each other, with special capes that came down in smart points below their waists in the same material. Pap said, the way the bodice underneath was bloused and the cape fitted so careful to show it underneath, the new dresses were fancier than what they wore before, and Mam and Martha might as well go to Atlantic City and roll up and down the boardwalk in one of Harry Hess's rolling chairs. But Mam and Martha didn't see it that way, and like the others, they took to wearing coverings all the time.

Mam didn't seem any happier for the new clothes, but if she thought she needed them to make up for sending Barb to Annie Musser's party, none of us was about to stop her. Pap wasn't pleased, though, the day a ramshackle wagon with a mule that belonged in a glue factory draggled down the lane, and Mammy and Martha gave the old black woman driving it their old clothes. It must have been good pickings for the Welsh Mountain people about then, with so many conversions and so many dresses being given away. The old woman in the wagon showed her gums, waving with one hand and slapping the reins with the other all the way out the lane. Pap watched her from the barnyard gate, shaking his head, while Martha and Mam waved back from the porch.

It was around then that Pap told us he'd chosen a headstone for Barbie. "I thought on it a bit," Pap said, "but now I know what I want it to say." He'd consulted with Hen, I knew, because the two of them had their heads together every day as soon as Hen got home from his school teaching. Pap had visited the marble works in New Holland and picked out a stone, but it was Hen who decided what should go on it. Pap wanted it to say more than Barbie's name and how old she was, and the deeper the revival got, the more he and Hen talked. Finally, Hen being a school teacher, Pap put it on him to make up a proper saying in verse. That took time, with Hen working out rhymes and Pap folding his arms and saying he didn't quite like them. The two of them kept pretty secret about the words they wanted, but soon after Martha joined church, Pap pulled out a paper one night after supper and told us what he wanted Mr. Storb to write on the stone.

> This spotless column o'er our sister's grave
> But marks the corner where her body lies,
> Her spirit bright unto the God that gave
> Has upward gone where pleasure never dies.

Martha started to cry when she heard it, leaning over so all we could see was her white cap in the lamp light. Mam cried, too, her head up and dabbling at her eyes with a hankie she pulled from under her cape. I tried to pretend I didn't have tears running down my cheeks too and rubbed my sleeves over them so it wouldn't show. But nobody noticed because we were all crying except Hen, who was looking out and away. Still, even he looked satisfied when Mam said it was right and beautiful to put on Barbie's stone. "I wanted you to think so, Mammy," he said. His face relaxed, and he looked less grim than he had since we'd heard about Barbie being killed. "It's just the truth," he added. Mam held out her arms, and he went over and hugged her. Hen started to cry then too, the first time I'd seen him act even human since the accident. He and Mam held onto each other until Pap cleared his throat.

Hen was ready to run right upstairs to his books, but Martha stopped him. "I like it, too, Hen," she said, her face sort of open and her eyes wide, the way she could look when she wasn't caught up in any convictions. If she'd looked like that more often, she would have been a beauty, but it was enough that Hen saw her. He stopped long enough to give her hand a squeeze. "It's right, Martha," he said before he turned away and tramped upstairs. The rest of us sat on, pulling ourselves together, I guess, till Mam said she had some mending to do and Martha could get on with the stockings she was knitting.

Moss's bad ear never bothered her times like that, and I knew how she hated to knit. She looked up real perky and said maybe it would be better to finish Barbie's quilt. Mam started to say how my old stockings were about worn out and I needed new ones, but Pap looked up from the paper with Hen's words on it. "I suspect Barbie's quilt is more important than Silas's feet," he said. "Silas, Mart, help your sister get the quilting frame set up in the light." Mart and I carried it out from the spare room where it had been shoved in a corner and helped her tighten the ratchets to stretch out the part she was working on, and Mam fetched the basket with the quilting thread. "It's time to get on with this," Martha said, settling down in front of the frame. She was threading the needle when Mart and Pap and I went out to work in the stripping room.

Stripping tobacco was the main work that kept us busy through the winter, Mart and Pap and me regularly, and Mam and Martha when they could spare time from women's chores and help, too. Hen looked in now and again, but mostly he spent his time on school teaching now and paid Pap two dollars a week room and board from his wages instead of working the farm, especially with Mart home and me out of school so we could get by without him. The stripping took most of the winter, working away in that warm, sharp little room with a swig of cider now and then to wash down the tobacco dust.

Stripping tobacco was tedious, I guess, except that you never did it alone, and that made the difference. Those were the times Sam and I talked, even if Charl and Hon were usually hanging around when we were at his place. Uncle Menno often enough left to see about repairing harness or doing some other chores once he saw we were settled and working, though he'd poke his head in now and then to check how we were getting on. Pap was more likely to be at Uncle Elias's, because he knew Uncle Elias needed the help and was usually behind with things unless his brothers gave him a hand.

That fall and winter Sam and I talked a lot about the revival, so even now the thought of it reminds me of the smell of the stripping room, sharp and strong and not very good to the nose until you got accustomed to it. Of course

Charl and Hon talked about it too, but we tried not to pay attention except when Hon said something so smart we only pretended not to listen to such a little kid.

One night over at Uncle Menno's we were talking about how many had joined church and how all you could see on the women's side since November was white caps on every head high enough to show above the bench back. "Like mushrooms growing out of dead bodies," I remember saying. I hadn't forgiven Martha for believing the visiting preachers and joining church, and Mam was so different I hardly knew her. Her dressing plain hadn't stopped her from crying into the night, only not quite as loud as at first. Thinking about what the revival had done to us, I asked Sam why all the women had gone crazy. Sam shook his head and kept on putting leaves into the stripping box. "Don't ask me, Sike," he said, looking at the leaves he was sorting as if they took all his attention.

That Charl never did know when to keep his mouth shut. "They don't want to go to hell like Barbie and Enos," he said, bold as you please. Usually I knew better than to let myself be riled by anything Charl could say, but for some reason he really got to me that time, and before I knew it I had him by the scruff of the neck and was shaking him so hard his feet pedaled in the air and his face got red. "Stop saying that, you blasted little parrot!" I remember yelling at him before I realized how tall I was and how little he was. As soon as I did, I thumped him onto the floor. He stood there for a minute. Then he started to bawl and shouted that I was a heathen and a bully. He must have seen that Hon was smiling, and that made him all the madder. "You'll all go to hell!" he shouted, and stamped his foot before he tore out of the stripping room.

We were quiet for a minute till Sam said, "He had it coming. When you had him up in the air I felt like taking a poke at him myself. You'd think he was a girl, the way he goes on about those preachers. He carries on about them more than Bess, and I can't figure out why."

"It's because he's as scared as they are," Hon piped up in that smart little voice of his, and Sam and I knew Hon was right. "Last night he told Pap he wanted to join church so he wouldn't go to hell," Hon said. I couldn't help asking what Uncle Menno said to that, and Sam grinned and said his Pap had told Charl that if he planned on getting to heaven he'd better start by getting on with his chores and he'd have plenty of time when he was old enough to know what he was doing.

"He probably will, too," Sam added, "but you wouldn't catch me ever joining a church that would do this kind of thing to Barbie." "Me either," Hon said, and Sam said, "What about you, Sike?"

I was going to say I'd get revived when hell froze over, but for some reason I stopped. Finding myself ready to half kill Charl had shaken me, I guess, because I'd felt like tearing him in pieces, but I wondered what Pap would have thought if he'd seen me. Even with the way he felt about the railroad, I could imagine the look on his face if he'd come on me like that. "Give me a couple more years to think about it," I said finally.

It was December before Uncle Elias got around to his butchering. I remember Mam shaking her head and saying only Elias would butcher in the moon's downgoing and he'd likely waited till it was so cold the meat would freeze and spoil. Pap said, "Now, Barbara. There are few enough of them at home now that they can afford to have the meat shrink some, and if it's a bit cold, the carcasses will cool down sooner and wouldn't have to hang so long. I never heard you fuss before about speeding up work." Pap didn't smile, but I could tell he was pleased to hear Mam fussing over anything, quiet and strange as she'd been since the accident. When she clicked her tongue and shook her head over the ways Elias managed things, it seemed almost like before.

Pap and Mart and I got up extra early and were over at Uncle Elias's well before light. Even so, Dave and Uncle Elias had already got started and stuck one of the pigs. We heard it squealing before we got there. Pap muttered that it didn't make that much difference in the bleeding out if you killed them before you stuck them and told us to hurry on. I was glad they'd done it before we got there, even though I knew there'd be another and a beef yet to go. Pap didn't like the killing either, but he said you did what you had to.

"They don't usually carry on that bad," Uncle Elias said when we got there, "but when they do, there's not much you can do about it." I started to gag and was afraid I was going to throw up, so I stepped back from the light and swallowed a few times, fighting it down. I saw that Mart and Dave had turned away, too. Somehow that made me feel better.

But there wasn't time to fuss over feelings. Uncle Elias had set water in the scalding trough the day before to swell the boards, and Aunt Annie and Biney had already started filling it with boiling water. Pap set me to carry out more water from the washhouse. I moved some, carrying buckets two at a time and helping Biney pump water to fill the kettles again for the second pig.

Biney was lively and jabbered away, so she seemed almost the way she used to, except that now she had her hair in a bun and a white net cap on. "I always like butchering days," she said. I could tell she meant it, if I couldn't see her face because the sun wouldn't be up for another hour or so. "Come on, Biney," I said. "How can you like killing things?"

"I don't think about that part," she said, cocking her head on one side. I couldn't help snorting and saying she'd think different if she had to watch the pigs get stuck. Biney looked away and nodded. "I hear them," she said, "but I don't think about it. I set my mind on things like ham and sausage and scrapple and all the food we'll get from it."

I could hardly believe what she was saying, when the last time I'd been alone with her she was in that much of a state, no one would have believed she'd ever talk sense again. I'd felt a million years old that day, like she was a kid having fits, but now here she was talking to me like I was the young one, and she'd never thought anything but what was practical and needed to be done. It hit me that conversion, white cap, and all, she was as much a catbird as ever.

"I'll call you when they're ready to kill the beef," I called to her before she got to the washhouse door with the last of the buckets. She whirled around so fast she slopped water on her skirt. "I'll be getting ready to put up the meat," she shot back at me. "I don't want to know."

"I'll be sure to call you!" I shouted back. Then I walked to the barn, knowing I'd tried to hurt her and half ashamed about it but feeling a kind of satisfaction that I'd made her remember where the food came from and that the killing came first.

That butchering there was as much bustle as ever, but no one was happy the way we used to be. Something was missing, and I knew it was Barbie and the way she and Biney would make us laugh with their carrying on. Mart had taken a pig tail and stuck a pin through it to play jokes with, but the tail stayed in his pocket, as if he hadn't the heart to pin it on anybody and play any pranks that would remind us of her.

As for Martha and Biney, they both seemed like strangers in their new dresses and caps. It didn't make so much difference with Martha, sober as she'd always been, but I still hadn't figured out what to make of Biney. That wide mouth of hers didn't look natural when it wasn't set in a smile or else going a mile a minute about some kind of nonsense. Now she was trying to be grown-up, I guess, like the new cap made her a woman in one step, if she did forget now and then and start running on in her old way till all of a sudden she'd remember and draw up like someone had twitched a rein. I tried teasing her some and asked had she seen Amos Landis lately, but she didn't rise to the bait. "I don't go to crushes any more," she said. "Besides, I never was much interested in him."

The one thing she did get off on, blabbering like she used to, was Mrs. Divet that looked after Grandmother. Biney started chattering to tell about how Mrs. Divet had taken to shuffling out to the biffy with Grandmother's dishes and dropping them down the toilet holes. "Mam wondered what was happening to them all," Biney said, enjoying the joke of it even from under her cap. "We lost half a dozen before I went out to sprinkle lime and saw what was down there."

I started to laugh and ask if they were going to keep those dishes for company, but Aunt Annie looked up from the pile of bones she was picking meat from, her face tired and tight looking. "It's not funny," she said real sharp. Biney's mouth was wide and droll, set to tell us more of Mrs. Divet's goings on, but it was like the rein had twitched and she remembered her cap after forgetting it half a minute. I stopped laughing, and Aunt Annie looked over to where Mammy was dipping lard into a crock.

"Barbara, I'm at my wit's end and have been for months. If there were more than Dave and Biney to help out, I could manage, but with only them I can't keep up with nursing Grandmother and Mrs. Divet, too, because she's more trouble now than Grandmother. And what with Dave wanting to get married and move off, I don't know what we're going to do."

"I've had her on my hands for fourteen years," Aunt

Annie wailed, "and I've never known all that time if the house would be standing in the morning or burnt down around our ears from that pipe of hers. If she wasn't lying there taking up half the house, Dave and Ella could settle here, but if he moves off someplace else, Elias won't be able to manage and we'll have to give up the farm. And you know with the prices and bad times, we don't have money to go anyplace else."

Mammy set down the ladle and straightened up, her face red as an apple from working in the heat. She turned to Aunt Annie and asked if Dave and Ella had found a place yet.

"He hasn't come up with a thing," Aunt Annie said, "but I'm afraid if he doesn't get married soon it'll be worse trouble."

Mam nodded and bent back to her ladle. "The boy needs to settle," she said. Before we went home that evening she told Aunt Annie she'd talk to Pap.

Mam always did what she said. First she talked to Pap and then Pap talked to Uncle Menno and Uncle John, and Uncle John talked to the Mellinger aunts. Aunt Mary finally said they could take Grandmother because there were more of them to help and keep an eye out she didn't burn the house, though Aunt Sue fussed, afraid of having to be Grandmother's nurse again after getting out from that when Mrs. Divet came and she moved to Uncle Menno's.

Soon as it was decided, Aunt Sue went house hunting and bought herself a place in Soudersburg with the money Granddad had left her, though everyone but Mam shook their heads over how she'd make out on her own. Pap was the one who talked with Grandmother. He said it broke his heart, the way she looked at him and said she'd lived in the home place since she was sixteen and was too old to change now when she was almost ninety. He said she rolled her head away then and just said, "*Macht nichts.*"

Through that winter it seemed as though we spent half our time at church. Around then they moved Sunday school from afternoons to mornings so you couldn't really miss going to it the way we mostly used to. I remember that year they kept it going through the winter, too, instead of just summers. It must have done what Bishop Eby had in mind, because people kept on joining church through that fall, and I noticed that Mam wouldn't get out the dandelion or elderberry wine for company any more unless Peter the Hermit was over and Pap sent her especially to fetch it from the cellar.

Martha and Biney had started going off together once a week to a Bible reading class some of the young people had started up. When it was Martha's turn to have it at our place, I remember Pap scratching his ear and saying it was some change from the last party, the knot of them sitting together in the parlor so quiet you couldn't hear them from the next room till they started singing " 'Tis the Harvest Time," the music ringing through the house. I didn't go in, though Martha asked me to, saying Mart and Sam and I could stand a good dose of the Bible. Even so, I have a picture in my mind of them sitting in a circle with their heads bowed. What I think of is the big German Bible lying closed on the parlor table beside the lamp while they studied their English verses.

I noticed Willis Shirk showed up with the rest of them, still dangling after Martha what chance he got, but she didn't invite him to dinner any more or let him come over by himself evenings. When Mart asked what had happened to her beau, Martha sniffed and said she couldn't take a man seriously who could entertain infant baptism.

We heard more from the railroad, too. When Pap didn't answer any of their letters, they sent a man to see us again. This one was older than the first one, a vice-president real high up come all the way from Philadelphia to have a talk with Pap. I could tell Pap was pleased they'd send someone so important that far, and he invited him into the parlor where they spent almost an hour before the man left again. Mammy kept wiping her eyes and trying to pretend she wasn't crying while he stayed, and Pap seemed especially serious the next few days, walking around with his arms folded and hardly noticing when anyone talked to him. He didn't seem mad the way he did earlier, more like he was thinking hard and turning his thoughts over and over. That was only a few weeks before Christmas, as I remember it, because Pap didn't tell us what the man said till Christmas day.

Usually we had a big Christmas, Enos and Bob and their families coming for dinner and Lizzie and Sarah and theirs staying over. This year, though, Mam said she hadn't the heart to celebrate, with Barbie in the grave. Enos and Bob and Lizzie all said they'd make out all right and take the chance to eat with other relatives, but Mam wanted Sarah. She said having her would be a comfort.

Sarah and John and their brood alone were enough to make a good-sized bunch besides Mam and Pap and Peter the Hermit and Mart and Hen and Martha and me, but everyone was pretty quiet over Christmas dinner, all of us thinking how it used to be and wishing Barbie was with us to cut up with the children and help with the serving and make us all laugh. Martha bustled around filling up platters, doing what she could to make up for Barb not being there. But hard as she tried, it wasn't much of a go. Every time I looked around it seemed like someone or other was taking a quick wipe at their eyes. It was a relief to push back from the table and let the women get on with washing up.

When the dishes were put away, Pap loaded us into the carriages to drive to Hershey's and see Barbie's stone. Hen took the buggy so he could go on from there to Annie Keene's and take over a present he had for her. He and

Annie were thicker than ever and we'd all got used to it, if Martha still fussed that any brother of hers could find a better woman than that. But she fussed over Enos and Bob's wives, too. The rest of us just figured Hen had made his choice.

It was a pretty drive, everything covered with snow that had melted some the day before and frozen again into a crust that sparkled in the sun like crushed glass. The trees were bare and lacy black, standing up here and there from the whiteness that covered up the fields and looked to go on and on farther than any of us could see. I couldn't help thinking how much Barb would have liked seeing it, with the eye she always had for what was pretty.

The graveyard looked pretty, too. First we drove on past the church to the old one where my little sisters were buried by the bush near the middle. Then we came back to the new one beside the church where Barbie was. With the snow like a white coverlet over everything, the graveyard looked of a piece with the country all around, the fields across the road and past the far end and the ones beyond the Pequea all so white you hardly saw the picket fence around it. The new graveyard hadn't been used very long, and there weren't many stones in it yet. It was easy to see the new one part way down, so white it was hardly darker than the snow. Walking beside old Peter Eby, Pap paused beside his pap's grave by the gate, then led us down the path and over to Barbie's grave, the rest of us picking our way behind him.

We walked slow because the snow was hard on top, and every step we broke through to the soft part underneath, all but Sarah's little ones who looked surprised when the crust broke and they had to stop and pull a leg out. John carried the next smallest boy, and Sarah had the baby wrapped up with a corner of the blanket folded over his face so he wouldn't mind the cold.

Pap and old Peter got to the stone first and stood looking at it while the rest of us bunched up around them. Pap had picked one that was thin and taller than it was wide. At the top it said "Sister" and had Barbie's name. Under that it said "Daughter of Peter and Barbara N. Hershey" and told when she died and how old she'd been. Under that in smaller writing was Hen's verse, the letters cut sharp and fresh and taking up more than four lines where there wasn't room to fit them across the stone. Pap told Hen to read it out, and Hen started to say it for us. "This spotless column o'er our dear sister's grave. . . ." He stopped and turned around, madder than a hornet. "That's not what I wrote," he said. "Who messed up my line?" Sarah said she thought it sounded nice the way it was, but Hen said it wasn't what he'd written and the meter was ruined. Mammy looked up, her eyes red from crying, and said Martha had especially wanted it to say "dear sister."

"That's what she was, too, our dear sister, and the stone should say it," Martha said, glaring at Hen over the hankie she had against her face. Then she started crying again, and Hen shrugged his shoulders.

"Read the rest of it," Sarah said, her voice so calm that Hen looked sheepish. "I'm sorry," he said to the rest of us but mostly to Mam, I suspect. "I have to keep these things in mind if nobody else around here does," he went on. "I'm thinking about going to the Normal School at Millersville next year."

"That so?" Pap said, raising his eyebrows, and Peter the Hermit asked if Hen didn't have enough English education already. "No, not enough," Hen said, "not yet." Pap looked at Barbie's stone with the verse cut into it and said he guessed he could spare him and it shouldn't make much difference to the farm, and Hen said, "Thanks, Pap." Then he cleared his throat and read the verse all the way through, his voice husky at first but strong and stubborn as if he was just daring anyone to say it wasn't so when he got to "Her spirit bright unto the God that gave, Has upward gone. . . ."

Mam and Martha were crying, and Sarah was patting the baby, her face bent against the blanket while she rocked him against her shoulder. Besides the sniffles, all you could hear when Hen finished was the quiet hushing sound she was making, something you wouldn't have noticed except in the sharp of the cold and the sunshine and the glitter from the snow. We bowed our heads.

When we put them up, we kept standing, as if no one wanted to move away and be the first to head to the carriages. Pap especially stood in front of the stone, his head still bowed while he stared at it, his arms folded. Finally Hen stamped his feet and said he had to get on to the Gap.

"Hang on a minute," Pap said. "I've been meaning to tell you what the railroad man said when he came by." Hen stopped and looked at Pap like the rest of us, because we'd all wondered what he and Pap talked about in the parlor. Pap looked up and said they'd had a good talk.

I couldn't help the bitterness that came out in me, and I said, "Did he say they were to blame for killing Barbie?"

"Easy, Sike," Mart said, and I shut my mouth, but Pap answered what I asked because he knew it was what we all wanted to know.

"Not exactly," Pap said. "He admitted the train was going too fast and if the engineer had been more careful it wouldn't have happened."

"We knew that already," Hen said. "What about the whistle. Did he admit they didn't whistle in time?"

"He said no one could know that for sure," Pap said, "because fast as the train was coming around the hill it was hard to know if it was before or after. But it wouldn't have made any difference." Mart and I looked at each other, and

I knew he thought that kind of talk was as much hogwash as I did, just another excuse, but we held our tongues.

"What else did he say?" Sarah's John asked. "Did he admit any responsiblity?"

"He did," Pap said. "He said that the railroad wasn't to blame in the eyes of the law, but that wasn't everything and they knew it. That's why they want to do something, he said, to show they knew their fault in the eyes of God."

We were all surprised to hear that the railroad could have a conscience. I might have made some smart remark, but Pap went on. He was looking out over the creek now and off into the distance. "He talked about the engineer, too, and said how he's taken on at what he did. He's just a young man, and his whole family's broken up about it. He still works for the railroad, but he won't touch an engine since the accident. He took it hard, the man said. It might ease him and his family some if we allowed that he didn't intend what happened."

I guess I exploded then. In spite of myself I burst out, "You mean he wants us to forgive them?" Instead of putting me in my place the way he should have, Pap gave me a funny look. I knew he knew as well as I did just how much that railroad man was asking us to do. "That's exactly what he wants of us, Silas."

We were all quiet while it sank in. Sarah was still rocking the baby, but she looked over his head and said in that quiet, steady voice of hers that it was a hard thing to ask but not more than our Lord does. "It's wrong to hold spites and be bitter," she said. "Forgiving may be the hardest thing we have to do, but it's no more than what our Savior asks."

John asked what kind of gesture they had in mind, and Pap said, "I told him flat out I wouldn't take money for Barbie's blood." He paused and looked at Peter Eby, as if he wanted some sign that what he'd done was right. Old Peter nodded, and Pap went on, "But he said something else would do, maybe if we took a free trip somewhere, he said, just as a sign that we knew they didn't intend it."

"We all know they didn't intend it," Hen said, "any more than governments intend wars, but wars happen and Barbie's dead."

"With our Lord," Sarah said softly.

"May the Lord give us strength to do what's right," Pap said. He stretched his arms as if he wanted to loosen a kink in his muscle and said it was time to be getting home. One by one we turned from Barbie's grave and walked to the carriages.

From there Hen drove to the Gap, and Sarah and John went straight to Weaverland so as not to make a double trip, but Peter Eby came back to supper with us. When we bowed our heads for the blessing, he surprised us by praying out loud and asking God to heal our family the way Jesus healed the man blind from birth.

"When His disciples asked if that man was being punished for sin, our Lord said he wasn't, and when they asked if he was being punished for his parents' sins, Christ said no again. He said the man's affliction was sent so that the works of God could be made manifest. Then he spit in the dust, covered the man's eyes, and sent him to wash off the clay. You know this family's affliction wasn't sent to punish but to show the love and forgiveness made manifest through our Lord Jesus Christ. We pray for them to be healed as our Lord healed the blind man when He sent him to wash in the holy pool of Siloam. We ask in Jesus' name, Amen."

Pap said amen too, and then we opened our eyes, passed around the platters, and ate the sliced meat and fresh bread and relishes Mammy and Martha had set for us.

XX.

Looking back after the years in between, that still seems like the longest one I ever lived through, and that winter like the longest winter. When the spring finally came, Mart packed his suitcase and went back out West, and Pap, Mam, and Martha took the trip the railroad offered to Niagara Falls.

I was the one who drove Grandmother from the home place over to Uncle Menno's. We made a bed for her in the box of the spring wagon, but the whole way over I don't remember her saying anything except, "I've lived there all my life," over and over in Dutch.

We got her settled in, but Aunt Mary took away her pipe and only let her smoke when someone was with her, and she didn't last long. She died on the last day of May, a month before Barbie's birthday. I remember old Peter Eby standing beside her grave and watching while they lowered her coffin in the front row of the graveyard beside my granddaddy. "Everything changes," old Peter said. It struck me he said it in English.

Even the revival died after a last spurt of conversions in January. It was as if people had all the changes they could take at once and put on the brakes in time to stop the whole Mennonite Church from turning Methodist. Amos Wenger showed up again in Lancaster that spring when the bishops called him down for breaking church rules with around a dozen series of meetings. After that he settled for a while in Millersville, but the local church didn't let him preach, and after a few years he packed off to Virginia to head a school there.

But not before he'd made changes. Church is a lot more important now than it was before I was grown-up, though I'm not sure the revival mightn't have scared as many out as got brought in, like Sam and Hon. They joined the United Brethren in Paradise. Charl was the only one of that batch who did join. He was even a preacher for a time, till he got kicked out of church for singing in the Paradise choir. Mart came home after his year out West, but he and Hen both turned Presbyterian. I guess Annie Keene led them both into it. She and Hen got married a couple years later and moved in at home to farm for Pap, though Hen kept on with his teaching, too. I have to say Annie made him a good wife, almost as bustly as Mam used to be before the accident, if she couldn't be as good at keeping everything in order.

Of course she had Martha to help, because Martha stayed home till later, fighting some with Hen when they shared the house but saying she overlooked his faults because he'd been led into them.

As for me, I married Lillie in 1905 and have been a good Mennonite ever since, or mostly, though they set me back from church a few times when someone spotted me going in for a nip at the Rising Sun.

I guess the new ways that came after Barbie got killed never took on me the way they did with the younger ones who couldn't remember any different.

Lillie and I had a long life together, but she's been gone for thirteen years and Martha for nearly two and almost everyone else who still remembers. After Martha went I had to give up the house, and it was arranged for me to stay here at Landis Homes. Lillie's mother was a Landis, so it's almost like I'm still with family, especially with Biney down the hall. She's likely to natter at me the way Martha used to and talk away same as usual. Biney's worn a covering almost seventy-five years, but I'm not sure the revival ever took completely on her, either. She's still a catbird.

But that's all past. Looking over the fields and seeing the color of another spring coming to them, I know I may not see another. I can't make out the new growth as well as I used to, and the green isn't so bright. Soon I'll be with Lillie, resting in our plot in the graveyard at Hershey's at the far end from Grandmother and halfway from Barbie and Martha and Mammy and Pap and the others. But I know that I'll be resurrected with them, too, through faith in our Lord Jesus Christ. I never worried over that, even before the revival.

AFTERWORD

Although I have worked from documented sources and have used historical names for most of the characters in my narrative, I have invented the action and the characterizations. Thus I imagined some as more or less unpleasant because fiction requires conflict and interaction, prejudice as well, in what I imagined Silas felt—or, rather, what I might have in his place. My grandfather, the real Silas, spoke of Barbie and of the accident all his life, but I never heard him cast blame.

Fictionalized though my study is, I first conceived it because Silas and Aunt Martha spoke of the accident so much. I spent years trying to find and fit together the pieces, becoming more and more convinced that the story needed to be told, a judgment confirmed by Mark Wenger's article in *Pennsylvania Mennonite Heritage* of April 1981 which examines the accident and subsequent revival and concludes with the comment that only one side of the story has been presented because the Lancaster County conservatives had no spokesman. Although I have not meant to be their apologist, I have tried to give them a voice and to articulate the opposition to the revival which existed in the county at the end of the last century.

Throughout my research I had unstinted help from Silas's children. Elsie Hershey Harsh and my cousin John gave me information about farming, about the accident, and about Bishop Isaac Eby, whose grandson Aunt Elsie married; Elizabeth Hershey Zimmerman and Uncle Elmer gave me books, pictures, and church information; Willis Hershey told stories that wound their way into my text; my mother, Evelyn Hershey Stambaugh, answered questions, and my father Clarence told me about farming; Lester Hershey lent me family pictures and the family Bible (the English one), and Aunt Mary showed me pictures from her family to illustrate nineteenth-century Mennonite dress. Reba Hershey Nolt gave me a portrait drawing of Barbie, and Doris Hershey Lowry gave me the finest compliment I have received on my manuscript. My sister, Nancy Stambaugh Retallack, and her husband Jack helped me with miscellaneous information, local geography, and everything else I asked them for.

Hershey and Eby blood runs beyond one or two generations, and I have not yet acknowledged my most important sources, Galen Hershey and the late Sabina Hershey Ranck. Galen gave me interview after interview, sharing with me his wonderful memory of the past, from details about Aunt Barbara's funeral to campaign slogans for the 1896 presidential race, while his wife Margie gave me coffee so that I could absorb all that Galen had to tell. The last time I visited him, Galen was pruning trees, and when I complimented him on his garden, remarked, "You know, you don't want much yard work when you're past ninety."

Aunt Sarah's family also helped. I met the wife of Aunt Sarah's grandson at a sale, and she stopped by the same evening with Weaver's *Mennonites of the Lancaster Conference*. Martin Eby, Aunt Sarah's youngest son, passed on a wealth of information, directly or through his charming geneology of Aunt Sarah's descendents with its memories and pictures and family stories. I have cribbed from it shamelessly. Among the others who have helped me, I owe a special debt to the late Mrs. Jacob Martin for kindly allowing me to consult the diary which her mother, Ella Leaman, kept during the year of the revival.

After my primary sources, the library acknowledgments go almost without saying: the Lancaster Mennonite Historical Library, the Mennonite Historical Library and Archives at Goshen College, the Conrad Grebel Library of the University of Waterloo, the Millersville University Archives, the Lancaster Public Library, the Rutherford Library of the University of Alberta, and the Landis Valley Farm Museum. In all of them I was received with courtesy and friendly help. Even the Baer's *Almanac* staff put themselves out to provide me with the help I needed. I also drew upon the Lancaster Historical Society.

To my many collaborators, I return sincere thanks, not least to Phyllis and Merle Good, whose keen eyes showed me what to prune from an unwieldly manuscript. The facts, memories, and help of my friends are not to be confused with my historical interpretations or fictionalized imaginings.